Fertile Ground for Murder

Fertile Ground for Murder

Stella Sinclaire and Steven Nimocks

Published by Three Notch Publishing (English), 2024.

FERTILE GROUND FOR MURDER

Book Cover by negrorichi@yahoo.com

First Edition. September 30, 2024

ISBN: 979-8227409218

Written by Stella Sinclaire and Steven Nimocks

Also by Stella Sinclaire

Thieves in Velvet
The Silent Sonata
Fertile Ground for Murder
Les Racines du Meurtre

Also by Steven Nimocks

Hidden in Plain Hue
Schizophrenia
The Elusive Isle
Thieves in Velvet
Desperate Remedies
Shattered Trust
The Last Librarian
Fertile Ground for Murder
Confiance Brisée
Les Racines du Meurtre
The Smart House
The Balance of Fear
The Core Directive
Help Desk

Watch for more at https://shortstorylovers.com/Steven-A-Nimocks4.

Table of Contents

To my lifelong spouse.

Epigraph

"The truth is rarely pure and never simple."

- Oscar Wilde

Acknowledgements

First, I wanted to thank my spouse for the support I received throughout this entire process.

My Alpha Readers were invaluable and provided much insight. Thanks to Melissa Nimocks, Steve Nelsen, Jacob Nimocks, Kacey Nimocks, Caston Smith and Heidi Paulson.

This project would never have been completed without the help of my editor, Steven Nimocks, at Three Notch Publishing.

Thanks to the Beta Readers at Entrada Publishing and Samantha Jay at Fiverr. They provided insights my Alpha Readers missed.

The cover designers' outstanding effort and hours of work led us to a solution. Thanks to negrorichi@yahoo.com and Razeel Hassan for their creative masterpieces.

A big thank you to Draft2Digital Publishing. Their platform made it almost too simple to accomplish the arduous task of indie publishing.

Prologue

The blue glow of the laptop screen cast sharp shadows across Samantha Brewer's angular face as she leaned back in her creaking office chair. Stacks of case files teetered precariously on the edge of the cluttered desk, threatening to spill their grim contents onto the dingy carpet. She rubbed at her gritty eyes, the ghost of a headache throbbing behind her temples.

On the screen, the waveforms of her latest podcast episode blipped and pulsed, her own raspy voice narrating the grisly details of a long-cold case.

"The victim, a 32-year-old accountant named Julia Marks," Samantha's recorded voice intoned, "was found in her apartment, strangled with the electrical cord of her laptop. Investigators initially suspected..."

Samantha tuned out her own words, her gaze drifting to the cramped confines of her studio apartment. Empty takeout containers littered the coffee table, their greasy scent mingling with the stale coffee and dust motes hanging in the air. Although it differed significantly from the tidy rural home of her upbringing, she took pride in owning it. A space carved out by sheer force of will, free from the cloying expectations and painful memories of her past.

A sudden chirp from her phone startled Samantha out of her reverie. She frowned at the unfamiliar number, the area code niggling at the back of her mind. With a sigh, she paused the podcast playback and swiped to answer.

"This is Samantha."

The distant voice was weak, but strangely familiar. Samantha's grip tightened on the phone, her heart stuttering in her chest.

"Willow Creek? What... what's going on?"

She listened intently, her expression shifting from confusion to disbelief to a sickening sense of dread. Her free hand clenched into a fist, the nails biting into her palm.

"When did this happen?" Samantha demanded, her tone sharpening. "Have the police... yes, of course. I understand."

Another pause, the static crackling over the line as Samantha squeezed her eyes shut, bracing herself against the desk with a white-knuckled hand.

"I'll be there as soon as I can. Let Delores know... tell her to hang in there. I'm on my way."

She ended the call; the phone slipping from her numb fingers to clatter on the desk. For a long moment, she simply stared into space, her mind reeling with the implications of what she'd just heard. Returning to Willow Creek, confronting the ghosts she had left... it was the last thing she wanted to do. But she had no choice. Not now.

With a heavy sigh, Samantha turned back to her laptop, methodically saving and closing her case files. She'd need to put her current investigations on hold and plan for her absence. Her listeners would understand - they knew she sometimes disappeared down the rabbit hole of a particularly complex case. They had no idea just how personal this one would be.

As she packed a small overnight bag, Samantha's gaze fell on a framed photograph gathering dust on her bookshelf. With trembling fingers, she plucked it from its perch, brushing away the cobwebs of memory.

A young girl grinned up at her from the faded Polaroid, her arm slung around the shoulders of a gangly young man. Samantha's unruly brown hair was pulled back in a sloppy ponytail, her face alight with laughter. Beside her, Ethan Green's green eyes sparkled with mischief, his smile wide and carefree.

He couldn't have been over 24 or 25, caught in a rare moment of joy during one of Samantha's first summer visits to Green Acres Farm. Before the distance, the silence, the slow drift of time and circumstance.

Samantha's heart clenched, a wave of nostalgia and apprehension washing over her. She'd spent so long running from her past, burying herself in other people's tragedies. But now... now it was time to confront the truth, no matter how painful it might be.

She tucked the photograph into her bag, a talisman against the darkness to come, and shoved the last box into her beat-up Honda Civic, the trunk groaning in protest. She wiped sweat from her brow and took one last glance at her tiny Chicago apartment, the peeling paint and dingy windows a stark reminder of the life she was leaving behind.

The endless ribbon of highway stretched before Samantha, the drone of the engine and the rhythmic thump of the tires on the asphalt, a hypnotic accompaniment to her tumultuous thoughts. She gripped the steering wheel; her knuckles pale against the worn leather, as the familiar road signs whipped by, each one a milepost drawing her relentlessly closer to Willow Creek.

Samantha's jaw clenched as the news of Ethan's death replayed in her mind, a macabre refrain punctuated by the reedy voice of the sheriff's deputy on the other end of the line. She could still hear the hollow ache in his tone, the unspoken apology for the burden he was placing upon her shoulders.

A pang of hunger gnawed at her empty stomach, and Samantha groped into the battered duffel bag on the passenger seat, her fingers closing around the smooth, cool skin of an apple. She drew it out, turning the fruit over in her palm as the sweet, earthy scent wafted up, rich with memories.

Samantha's throat constricted as she raised the apple to her lips, taking a crisp bite. The tart flavor transported her back across the decades to a simpler time, when the world was small and safe, cradled in the embrace of Green Acres Farm.

The image of the sprawling orchard, with its golden autumn light and abundant trees heavy with ripe red fruit, was vivid in her mind as if it had happened just yesterday. A tiny hand, dwarfed by Ethan's calloused fingers, as he led her between the gnarled trunks, his gentle voice spinning tales of the land's rich history.

Samantha blinked, and she was four years old again, perched securely in the circle of Ethan's arms as he boosted her up to pluck a shiny apple from a high branch. Her childish laughter rang out, pure and unrestrained, as she brandished her prize aloft in triumph.

"Look, Ethan! I got it!"

The corners of his eyes crinkled with affection as he set her down, crouching to meet her gaze. "You sure did, Sammie." He reached out, taking the apple from her small hands with a reverence that seemed at odds with the simple fruit. "You know, this apple is special. It's from the very first tree my grandpa planted when he started this farm."

Samantha's eyes widened. The apple transformed with a mythic quality in her young mind. She cradled it close, watching in rapt fascination as Ethan produced a well-worn pocketknife and deftly sliced the apple in two. He offered one glistening half to her, and they settled together in the dappled shade of the ancient tree, the sweet juice staining their smiles.

As they ate, Ethan's deep voice wove the tapestry of the farm's origins, of the hard-won battles against drought and pests, of the perseverance that had transformed his grandfather's humble plot into the thriving acreage surrounding them. His dreams for the future shone through - the desire to nurture the land, to cultivate life in harmony with nature's rhythms.

The memory faded like a wisp of smoke, and Samantha clutched the dry, fibrous core of the apple in her palm, the last vestige of its fleeting sweetness lingering on her tongue. She drew in a shuddering breath, blinking back the prickle of tears as the empty country road blurred before her eyes.

Samantha tossed the apple core out the window and settled her hands on the wheel once more, her jaw set in a grim line of determination. Whatever dark truths lay waiting for her in Willow Creek, Samantha would confront them head-on. For Ethan's sake, if nothing else.

The relentless miles continued to unspool before her, drawing her home. The memory flickered and faded, but its bittersweet ache lingered, a hollow throbbing in Samantha's chest. She blinked away the stinging moisture in her eyes, her grip tightening on the steering wheel as she navigated the winding interstate.

Up ahead, a small funeral procession crawled along the service road, the sleek black hearse leading a somber trail of mourners. Samantha's breath caught in her throat as she watched the melancholy parade, and her mind drifted back to that long-ago day when she had been swathed in black, a tiny, grieving figure adrift in a sea of well-meaning condolences.

The memory washed over her, vivid and raw...

Five-year-old Samantha perched on the weathered porch steps, her small body hunched in on itself as she tried in vain to stifle the hitching sobs. Her black dress, hastily donned that morning, felt stiff and scratchy against her skin, the unfamiliar fabric only compounding her discomfort.

Delores had tried coaxing her with soothing words and gentle embraces, but Samantha shrugged off her mother's ministrations, curling deeper into her cocoon of grief. Nothing could fill the vast, aching void that her father's absence had carved into her world.

The crunch of footsteps on gravel drew her gaze upward, her vision blurred by a fresh wave of tears. Ethan's lanky form resolved itself before her, his suit jacket draped over one arm as he settled onto the step beside her.

"Hey, Sammie." His deep voice washed over her, the familiar timbre a balm against the rawness of her sorrow. Without a word, he slipped an arm around her small shoulders, drawing her against the solid comfort of his side.

Samantha turned her face into the coarse fabric of his shirt, her tears dampening the crisp cotton as the floodgates opened once more. "I miss Daddy," she hiccuped, the words muffled and plaintive. "Why did he have to go away?"

She felt the rumble of Ethan's sigh, the gentle squeeze of his arm as he struggled to find the right words. "Sometimes, people have to go to heaven, even when we want them to stay with us," he said at last, his tone thick with shared grief. "But your daddy will always watch over you, Sammie. He'll always be in your heart."

Samantha raised her head, her small face crumpled with confusion and heartache. "But who's going to take care of me and Mommy now?" The question hung in the air, heavy with childlike worry.

Ethan's calloused fingers brushed away the tears streaking her cheeks, his touch achingly tender. "You've got your mommy, and she's one of the strongest people I know," he murmured. "And you've got me, too. I promise I'll always be here for you, Sammie."

A flicker of hope kindled in Samantha's eyes as she peered up at Ethan, her small hand fisting in the fabric of his shirt. "But don't you have a mommy and daddy to take care of you?" she asked, her voice wavering.

Ethan's sad smile held a world of loneliness and loss. "No, sweetie," he replied gently. "My mommy and daddy are in heaven, too. But you know what? When I need someone to lean on, I go to your mommy. She's always there for me, just like she's there for you."

Understanding blossomed on Samantha's tear-stained face as she nodded thoughtfully, the simple wisdom of Ethan's words taking root. "We all have to have someone to lean on," she echoed, her voice a mere whisper.

"That's right, Sammie." Ethan pulled her close once more, resting his cheek against her tousled hair. "And I'll always be someone you can lean on, no matter what."

The memory dissolved like a wisp of smoke, leaving Samantha adrift in the present once more. She drew in a shuddering breath, the phantom scent of Ethan's shirt mingling with the musty air of the car's interior.

As the funeral procession faded from view in her rearview mirror, Samantha felt the weight of Ethan's promise settle over her like a mantle. He had been her steadfast rock; her harbor in the storm for as long as she could remember. And now, as she steeled herself to confront the circumstances of his death, she knew she would carry the strength of his memory, his unwavering devotion, with her every step of the way.

The dusty bell above the convenience store door jangled as Samantha stepped inside, her boots scuffing against the worn tile floor. The familiar mingling of aromas—stale coffee, cheap beer and sour disinfectant—assaulted her senses, transporting her back to countless childhood pit stops during road trips with her family.

She made her way to the counter, fishing a crumpled bill from the depths of her jeans pocket as the bored-looking attendant eyed her with disinterest. "Fill up on pump two, please," Samantha muttered, sliding the money across the scratched Formica.

With a curt nod, the attendant pocketed her cash and hit a button, the harsh buzz of the ancient pump springing to life outside. Samantha turned on her heel and headed back out into the sweltering summer afternoon, squinting against the glare of the sun.

As she gripped the worn plastic handle and guided the nozzle into her car's gas tank, her gaze drifted across the expanse of the weathered gas station. A cluster of rusting, antiquated tractors dotted the overgrown field beside the building, their once-vibrant colors faded by decades of exposure to the elements.

A pang of nostalgia tightened Samantha's chest as she took in the familiar sight, memories of her childhood summers spent at Green Acres Farm flickering to life with each familiar detail.

She could almost hear the echo of Ethan's rich laughter, mingling with the distant drone of cicadas in the tall grass...

"Sammie! Over here, come look at this."

Nine-year-old Samantha whirled at the sound of Ethan's voice, her bare feet kicking up puffs of dust as she scampered across the sunbaked field toward him. He was crouched beside an ancient, rusted-out tractor, its once-glossy green paint chipped and faded to a sickly olive hue.

Ethan straightened as she approached, his brow furrowed beneath the brim of his tattered baseball cap. "Looks like the old girl has given up on me again," he sighed, swiping a calloused hand across his brow.

Samantha frowned, peering at the decrepit machine with a critical eye. "Can't you just buy a new one, Ethan?" she asked, her small voice laced with exasperation. "This one's always breaking down."

A rich chuckle rumbled from Ethan's broad chest as he shook his head, his green eyes crinkling with amusement. "It's not that simple, Sammie," he replied, beckoning her closer with a wave of his hand. "This tractor has been a part of the farm for a long time. It's got history, and it's my job to take care of it."

He motioned for her to join him as he swung open the tractor's rust-streaked hood; the hinges protesting with a shrill creak. "See, when something's broken, you don't just throw it away," Ethan explained, his deep voice taking on the gentle, patient cadence he reserved solely for her. "You try to fix it, to understand what's wrong and make it right."

Samantha watched, transfixed, as Ethan's hands deftly navigated the tangle of greasy machinery, his fingers plucking and prodding with the ease of long practice. "But what if you can't fix it?" she couldn't help but ask, her young mind already grappling with the complexities of Ethan's philosophy.

Ethan paused, his piercing gaze finding hers as a warm smile tugged at the corners of his mouth. "Then you learn from it," he replied, straightening to his full height and beckoning her closer still. "You take what you can, and you use that knowledge to improve things in the future."

He rested a broad hand on her slender shoulder, giving it a gentle squeeze. "It's not just about the tractor, Sammie," Ethan continued, his voice taking on a weight that seemed to stretch beyond the confines of the ramshackle farm. "It's about life. There will be times when things break down, when people let you down. But you can't give up on them. You have to try to understand, to fix what you can, and to learn from what you can't."

The words settled over Samantha like a warm blanket, their profundity belied by Ethan's simple, matter-of-fact delivery. She nodded slowly, absorbing the weight of his wisdom as she plucked a wrench from the battered toolbox at his feet.

"Here, let me help," she murmured, already clambering up onto the rusted footplate to peer into the tractor's murky depths.

The memory flickered and faded like an old home movie reel, the distant echoes of laughter and cicadas giving way to the low hum of the gas pump. She plucked the nozzle from the fuel tank and slipped it back into its cradle, the dull thunk of the pump's automatic cut-off echoing across the cracked asphalt.

As she slid back into the driver's seat, her eyes strayed one last time to the cluster of tractors, sentinels standing vigil over the forgotten detritus of the past. A faint smile tugged at the corners of her mouth, her fingers brushing against the worn denim covering her thigh.

Ethan would want her to try. To fix what she could, to learn from what she couldn't. It was the sole solution.

The engine rumbled to life beneath her, pulling Samantha back into the unstoppable movement of the present. With a steadying breath, she eased the car back onto the highway, her jaw set in grim determination as the road curved ever deeper into the heart of Willow Creek.

Chapter 1

The call had come two days ago, a voice from her past pulling her back to the place she'd sworn she'd never return. Willow Creek, Iowa. Population 5,241. And now, one fewer.

Ethan Green was dead. Murdered in cold blood out on his organic farm. The news had hit Samantha like a punch to the gut, stirring up a swirl of memories and emotions she'd long suppressed. Ethan, the golden boy of Willow Creek. The dreamer, passionate about changing the world, one pesticide-free tomato at a time.

Now he was gone, and the town was reeling. Samantha knew she had to go back, despite her instincts. She needed to discover the fate of her ex-neighbor and childhood idol. She owed Ethan that much. As Samantha grew up, Ethan served as both uncle and mentor, not just a friend.

The humid Iowa air slapped Samantha in the face as she stepped out of her car six hours later, stiff and bleary-eyed from the long drive. Her childhood home loomed before her, the faded yellow farmhouse now choked with overgrown weeds and sagging gutters. The porch swing creaked sadly in the breeze, one chain rusted through.

Samantha steeled herself and marched inside, the musty scent of neglect and mothballs overwhelming. She'd deal with the house later. Right now, she needed sustenance and intel, in that order, and headed across town.

Mae's Diner mirrored Samantha's memories precisely—a cheap haven of pink vinyl booths and black-and-white checkered floors, the mouthwatering aroma of fried chicken and apple pie permeating the air.

"Well, well, well! Samantha Brewer, back in person!"

"Hi Mae," Samantha wheezed, extricating herself with some difficulty. "It's been a while."

"I'll say! What's it been, ten years? Twelve? You're too skinny, girl. Sit yourself down, I'll fix you up."

Despite her bone-tiredness and the queasy churn of unease in her gut, Samantha found herself squeezed into a booth, a heaping plate of chicken fried steak and mashed potatoes swimming in gravy plopped in front of her.

Samantha dug in, letting the comforting flavors briefly blot out the gnawing grief. But she couldn't block out the low murmurs from the table of elderly farmers behind her.

"Such a shame about that Ethan Green fellow. Stabbed to death, right there in his cabbage field. What's this world coming to?"

"Organic farming is fine, but I always wondered if Ethan was trying to fix something that didn't need fixing. We have followed the traditional way for generations and it worked just fine. But I guess that modern mindset left some folks dissatisfied with the old methods."

Samantha's fork froze halfway to her mouth. Stabbed to death? In a cabbage field? The details hit like icy water in her veins, shocking her out of the cozy nostalgic haze.

She signaled for the check and dashed out, desperate for air. In a daze, she drove the familiar winding road out to Green Acres Farm, hands clenched bloodless on the wheel.

The fields that had once held neat rows of vegetables now stood fallow and yellowing, weeds already choking out the furrows. Yellow police tape fluttered around the perimeter, a macabre contrast to the pastoral scene.

A gruff deputy in a sweat-stained uniform waved her away from the entrance. "Sorry, miss, this is an active crime scene. I'm going to have to ask you to leave."

Samantha nodded, her mind racing, as she cautiously edged her car into reverse. She couldn't just sit idle, not this time. She needed someone in this town she could still trust, someone who could help her make sense of this nightmare...

Fifteen minutes later, Samantha walked into the Willow Creek Chronicle, the battered sign hanging askew above the entrance. The sharp, inky smell of newsprint assaulted her nose, mingling with old coffee and dust.

And there, hunched over a messy desk in the corner, was Jennifer Mack, Samantha's childhood best friend, scribbling furiously on a steno pad. Jen looked up and did a double take, jaw dropping open.

"Sam? Is that really you?" She rushed over and grabbed Samantha in an awkward hug. "Wow, I didn't know you were back in town! What are you doing here?"

Samantha pulled back, mustering a weak smile. "Hey Jen. As soon as I heard about Ethan, I came. I just... It's unbelievable. I need to discover what happened to him."

Jenny's expression darkened. "It's awful. The whole town is in shock. Look, why don't we grab a drink tonight and catch up? I'll fill you in on what I know."

"Deal. You still know all the dirt in this place?"

Jen scoffed. "In Willow Creek? I could fill an encyclopedia."

As the sun began its slow descent, painting the flat fields in streaks of orange and pink, Samantha and Jenny settled into a sticky booth at Rusty's Bar, nursing watery beers.

Joe Novak, former high school football hero, turned paunchy bartender, sauntered over, eyes widening in recognition.

"Well well, if it isn't Samantha Brewer, the big city hotshot. I didn't expect I'd see your face in here again. What brings you back to our humble abode?"

Samantha leaned in, flashing a wry smile. "Oh, you know Joe, just a little unfinished business. I'm sure a man about town like yourself has heard fascinating rumors lately..."

Joe's chest puffed out, his balding head gleaming under the neon beer signs. "Now that you mention it, I may have heard something. But I'd hate to spread gossip..." He trailed off, eyeing Samantha expectantly.

She sighed and pulled a twenty from her wallet, sliding it across the bar. "Cut the malarkey, Joe. What do you know about Ethan Green stirring up trouble before he died?"

Joe pocketed the bill with a smirk. "You didn't hear it from me, but word is Ethan was ruffling a lot of feathers with that tree-hugger organic stuff. Trying to get folks to switch over, badmouthing the big commercial farms. Let's just say he wasn't making many friends."

Samantha digested this as Joe sauntered away, turning back to Jenny with a frown. "So Ethan angered people left and right with his whole save-the-earth crusade? That could be a motive for murder."

Jenny took a long swig of beer, wiping her mouth. "He always was a stubborn mule. But who would actually kill him over vegetables? It just doesn't add up."

Samantha drummed her fingers on the table, mind churning. "I need to go to the source. Jen, how would you feel about teaming up again for old times' sake? Put those journalistic instincts to use?"

Jenny grinned. "Oh yeah! Samantha Brewer and Jenny Mack, together again? Willow Creek won't know what hit it."

An hour and another round later, Samantha pulled into the pristine driveway of 115 Oak Street, the lavish white Victorian home of her overbearing mother. Delores Brewer was the sole family Samantha had left behind all those years ago.

She'd barely made it to the porch before the door flew open and Delores came tottering out, a vision in a puff-sleeved floral blouse and pink curlers.

"Samantha Jean Brewer, get over here and give your mother a hug this instant!" She held out soft, perfumed arms and Samantha reluctantly sank into them, inhaling the familiar scent of White Diamonds and cherry pipe tobacco.

"Hi Mom. It's been a while."

"It certainly has, young lady! Now get in here. I just baked your favorite cherry pie!"

Samantha allowed herself to be guided into the doily-covered, flower-scented interior, where she settled uncomfortably on the edge of a horsehair sofa as Delores puttered around the kitchen.

"Now tell me, dear, how is your love life? A beautiful girl like you must be beating them off with a stick in that big city!" Delores set down a plate piled high with glistening pie and leaned forward, eyes avid.

Samantha squirmed and took a big bite, avoiding answering as she said, "Oh, you know, Mom, I've really been focused on my career..."

"Mm-hmm, that's what they all say. Well, no matter. I know several eligible young men around here who would be a perfect match for you!"

Samantha nearly choked on her pie. "That's very thoughtful, Mom, but I'm just here for a visit. I don't need you setting me up with half the county."

"Nonsense! Now, while you're here, I insist you stay in the guest room. I won't take no for an answer." Her expression turned sly. "Besides, then I can ensure you actually go out on some of those dates."

Samantha sighed and nodded, resigned to her fate. Hurricane Delores was indisputable.

Later, lying awake in the chintz hellscape of the guest room, Samantha stared at the water-stained ceiling, memories of her father threatening to overwhelm. His deep belly laugh as he tossed her in the air. The scratch of his stubble when he kissed her cheek. The ragged gasps of his last breaths in that hospital bed.

She squeezed her eyes shut and forced the memories down. She couldn't afford to fall apart, not now. Ethan needed justice. And somehow, she would be the one to get it for him.

Morning dawned gray and dreary, a perfect match for Samantha's sleep-deprived state. Guzzling coffee from Delores' fussy porcelain teacups, Samantha steeled herself and headed for the police station.

Sheriff Emmet Cooper looked like he'd stepped straight out of a Western, all leathered skin and suspicious squint. He eyed Samantha's proffered business card like it might turn rabid and bite him.

"True Crime Files, eh? Let me guess, you want to intrude here and stick your nose where it doesn't belong in the name of 'journalism'?"

Samantha widened her Bambi eyes. "I just want to help, Sheriff. Ethan was an... old friend. And my podcast has a lot of experience with cases like this. I promise I won't get in the way."

Cooper harrumphed into his walrus mustache, but Samantha could see him weakening. The murder of the town's most controversial resident was big news. He could use the publicity.

"Fine. I'll give you the broad strokes. But this is still an ongoing investigation, you hear? You put one toe out of line and I'll hogtie ya quicker than a fox in a henhouse."

Samantha nodded solemnly, her most earnest "who, me?" expression firmly in place as she pulled out a pen and notepad. But the Sheriff's gruff demeanor and thinly veiled hostility triggered a gnawing unease.

Silence ensued as the Sheriff just stared at Sam almost without blinking. Sam got creeped out as the silence lingered like a foul odor on a breezeless day.

Sam couldn't figure out what he was doing. Did he change his mind?

Chapter 2

The metallic squeaks of Sheriff Emmet Cooper's desk chair punctured the tense silence as he leaned back, still eyeing Samantha Brewer with unmasked skepticism. She shifted in the hard plastic seat across from him, the cluttered desk a no-man's-land between them.

Cooper swiveled back and forth, creating another squeak from his chair, his bushy mustache twitching. "Fine, Miss Brewer, but let me remind you - no meddling in matters that don't concern you."

Samantha locked eyes with him. "I grew up here, Sheriff. Ethan Green was an old friend. And I think there's more to his death than meets the eye."

Cooper harrumphed, "Well, ain't that a coinkydink? I was just thinkin' the same thing."

He reached into a battered file cabinet and pulled out a slim manila folder, slapping it on the desk. "Homicide file, knock yourself out."

Samantha eagerly flipped it open, only to grimace at the grainy 4x6 photos that slid out. They showed Ethan Green splayed amongst neat rows of cabbages, eyes staring vacantly at the sky. The front of his flannel shirt was stained a glistening crimson.

She swallowed hard and forced herself to examine the images clinically, the way she would any other case. "No defensive wounds or footprints were around the body, despite the morning rain. And what's that in his hand?"

Cooper leaned over, jabbing a thick finger at the photo. "That'd be the murder weapon. One of them fancy Japanese vegetable knives, sharp as a scalpel. We traced it back to Green's own kitchen."

Samantha frowned, saying, "Seems an odd choice for a suicide. The majority would opt for something quicker and cleaner."

"My thoughts exactly," and the Sheriff stood, pacing the small office like a caged bear. "Plus, no fingerprints on the blasted thing - not even Green's own."

"So you believe someone staged the scene?" It wasn't a question. Samantha's mind churned, puzzle pieces slotting into place. "Someone staged Ethan's death to look like a suicide."

Cooper nodded grimly. "It's a workin' theory. But I gotta explore all angles, ya know? Can't rule out suicide completely just yet."

Samantha bit her lip, an idea taking shape. She reached into her messenger bag and pulled out a slightly crumpled press pass, flashing the laminated square at Cooper like a talisman.

"Let me help, Sheriff. My podcast has a huge following - I've got resources, contacts. I can contribute to this investigation."

Cooper scowled, bushy brows furrowing like agitated caterpillars. "This ain't no game, missy. I can't have you runnin' around playin' Nancy Drew, muddyin' up my crime scenes."

"I would never—" She took a calming breath. "Look, Ethan was important to me—to this whole town. His family deserves answers, and I want to help find them. I promise to follow your lead, not step on any toes."

The Sheriff stared her down, pale eyes inscrutable. Samantha held his gaze, unflinching. Finally, Cooper threw up his hands in resignation.

"Aw, shucks. I must be goin' soft in my old age." He yanked open a filing cabinet and pulled out a thick manila folder, plopping it unceremoniously in Samantha's hands. "Copies of everything we got so far - crime scene reports, autopsy findings, witness statements. Knock yerself out."

Samantha clutched the file to her chest like a hard-won prize. "Thank you, Sheriff. I promise I won't let you down."

"Don't make me regret this, Brewer." Cooper stabbed a beefy finger in her direction. "My rep is on the line too. Let's just see if that fancy degree o' yours is worth the paper it's printed on."

Samantha was already poring over the documents, barely registering the backhanded jab. She flipped through grainy crime scene photos, coroner reports dense with medical jargon, hastily scrawled witness statements. It was exactly the type of puzzle her mind yearned to solve.

Lost in thought, she startled when Cooper cleared his throat impatiently. "If yer done snoopin', some of us got genuine work to do."

"Right, of course." Samantha stood, tucking the folder under her arm. "I'll let you know if I turn up any leads."

"You do that." The Sheriff's tone held a note of warning. "And Brewer, watch yer step round here. In a small town, secrets got a way of sneakin' up on ya from behind when ya least expect."

With that cheerful parting thought, he waved her out of his office. Samantha emerged into the hustle of the small police station, mind already whirring.

Her first stop was the evidence board - a cluttered collage of maps, timelines, and grainy suspect photos. She glanced around furtively before snapping a few covert shots with her phone camera.

A familiar twinge of excitement unfurled in her gut-the thrill of the chase. Samantha knew that feeling well - it had fueled her rise to podcasting fame, the dogged pursuit of truth against all odds.

She had a feeling she'd need every ounce of that tenacity to crack this case. Ethan Green had been Willow Creek's outspoken agricultural reformer, passionate and driven. Who would want him dead?

The Sheriff's words echoed in her mind as she strode out into the blinding Iowa sunlight. Watch your step around here.

Even cornfields in Willow Creek had eyes. And they were all watching her now.

Jenny Mack was waiting in their usual booth at Mae's Diner, flipping through a dog-eared copy of the Willow Creek Chronicle. She glanced up as Samantha slid in across from her, the cracked vinyl squeaking.

"You look worse than usual," Jenny said by greeting, taking in Samantha's disheveled appearance. "Guess your meeting with Cooper went well?"

Samantha snagged a chili cheese fry from Jenny's plate, ignoring her squawk of protest. "Oh, he's a regular Prince Charming. But he agreed to let me consult on the case."

"You don't say? Must be desperate." Jenny lowered her voice to a conspiratorial whisper. "People are spooked, Sam. An ugly murder like that, here? Folks ain't used to that kinda thing."

Samantha leaned in, pulling out the thick case file. "Perhaps you can help me make sense of this, then." She spread the crime scene photos across the Formica tabletop like a macabre jigsaw puzzle.

Jenny blanched, pushing away her half-eaten lunch. "Hey, warn a girl before you pull out the gore shots."

"Sorry." Samantha tapped a photo meaningfully. "Look here - see how the blood splatter doesn't match a self-inflicted wound?"

Her friend squinted at the image, then shrugged. "Looks like Rorschach test to me. You sure you're not reaching?"

Samantha shook her head vehemently. "Jen, I've been covering cases like this for years. I know staged crime scenes, and this fits the bill."

She shuffled through the paperwork, pulling out an autopsy diagram. "The angle of the knife wounds, the lack of hesitation marks. It reads like a cold, efficient kill."

Jenny held up her hands in surrender. "Alright, alright, I defer to the expert. So where does that leave us?"

Samantha chewed her lip, mind racing. "It leaves us with a town full of secrets and potential suspects. I must dig into Ethan's life to uncover who had the motive to kill him."

As if summoned, the diner door bell jangled and Mae bustled over with a coffeepot. "You gals plannin' to pay rent on that booth? Refills?"

They obligingly held out their mugs for a top-off. Samantha leaned in casually.

"Actually Mae, maybe you could help us out. We were just talking about Ethan Green and all the ruckus he'd been stirring up before he died. You must've heard things, serving the coffee and pie circuit."

Mae froze, eyes darting furtively around the busy diner. "Oh, honey, you know I don't like to gossip..."

"C'mon Mae," Jenny wheedled, flashing her most winning smile. "Just between us gals. We're trying to understand what happened to Ethan. For the family's sake."

The older woman wavered, clearly torn. She was just opening her mouth to reply when the bell jangled again. Mae blanched, the coffeepot trembling in her hand.

"Delores, what a surprise! You're not usually in this late..."

Samantha twisted around to see her mom sweeping into the diner, a vision in mint green and pearls. She made a beeline for their booth, a sweet smile on her face that didn't quite reach her eyes.

"Oh, what an unexpected treat, my two favorite girls together again! Samantha dear, budge over and make room for your mom."

With the deftness of a politician, Delores wedged herself in next to Samantha, forcing her to gather up the crime scene photos. Mae seized the chance to escape, scuttling away with a mumbled excuse about the lunch rush.

"Now then," Delores turned the full force of her attention on Samantha, eyes bright and avid in her powdered face. "I saw the sheriff's car outside. Don't tell me our girl is in trouble with the law again?"

"No, mom. And if you hadn't noticed, Deputy Connors is over there in the corner eating his lunch."

Delores turned to see, "Oh."

"And what do you mean, again?" Samantha bristled, cheeks flushed. "Mom, that was one time in high school."

Jenny raised an eyebrow, but refrained from commenting. Delores waved a dismissive hand. "Oh, I'm just teasing, pumpkin. But really, what business could you possibly have at that dreary jailhouse?"

There was a subtle barb beneath the words, a genteel disapproval. Her tone made it clear she'd already heard through Willow Creek's reliable gossip chains about Samantha's visit to the sheriff's station earlier. Samantha resisted the urge to squirm like an errant child.

"If you must know, I've offered to consult on Ethan Green's case. Lend my professional expertise."

"Your expertise." Delores' smile tightened at the corners. "Well, I'm unsure how much those urban skills will apply here in Willow Creek. We handle things a bit differently around here."

Samantha gritted her teeth. "Mom, someone murdered Ethan. This town should welcome anyone who wants to help find his killer."

Delores tutted, "Always so dramatic, Samantha. Tragic as Ethan's death is, I hardly think wild accusations will help. You'll only stir up more pain and trouble."

Her gaze turned meaningful. "If you really want to honor Ethan's memory, maybe you should focus on mending fences closer to home. Lord knows there's plenty that needs fixing in this family."

With that loaded proclamation, Delores stood, smoothing the wrinkles from her skirt. "Think on it, dear. I only want what's best."

She sailed out of the diner, leaving a cloud of White Diamonds and unspoken reproach in her wake. Samantha sank down in the booth, completely worn out.

Jenny let out a low whistle. "My word, Hurricane Delores hasn't lost her touch."

"That woman could give a master class in emotional manipulation." Samantha scrubbed a hand over her face, saying, "She never changes."

"Hey. Don't let her get in your head, okay?" Jenny reached across the table to squeeze her hand. "You're here to find the truth, not play happy families."

"Yeah. You're right." Samantha mustered a warm smile. "Okay, no more lollygagging. It's time to really explore this."

She cracked her knuckles and flipped open her notebook with renewed determination. "First: I think it's time I had a proper chat with the grieving sister. Let's hear what Natalie Sandoval has to say for herself."

Chapter 3

The iced latte grew tepid as Samantha Brewer tried not to fidget under Natalie Sandoval's piercing gaze. The trendy coffee shop was all exposed brick and reclaimed wood, a jarring contrast to Natalie's sleek business attire.

Samantha leaned forward, her best earnest-journalist expression firmly in place. "Thank you for meeting with me, Ms. Sandoval. I realize this must be a difficult time."

"It's Doctor, actually." Natalie's tone could have chilled a polar bear. "And I'm not sure what you hope to gain from dredging up ancient history, Miss Brewer. My brother and I were hardly close."

"Please, call me Samantha." She smiled, undeterred. "And I'd argue that your shared history is crucial to understanding what happened to Ethan. The complex family dynamics can often hold the key to a case like this."

Natalie's lips thinned. "Complex. That's certainly one way to put it."

She sat back, crossing her arms. "Fine. You want the sordid tale of the Green siblings? Buckle up."

"Ethan and I were like oil and water from the start. I, the studious one, always with my nose in a book, had a strong desire for success. And Ethan? That boy lived in his own little wonderland, convinced he could save the world one organic radish at a time."

Natalie huffed a mirthless laugh. "Our poor parents didn't know what to do with him. They'd find him in the fields, talking to plants, obsessing over compost. Meanwhile, I was building my first spreadsheet and researching the stock market."

Samantha nodded, scribbling in her notebook. "So you took unique paths."

"Understatement of the century." Natalie pulled out her phone, flipping through photos with an efficiency bordering on violence.

She thrust the screen toward Samantha. It showed a young boy with familiar green eyes, his face pressed against the trunk of an oak tree in some kind of embrace. In the background, a teenage girl with a blonde ponytail bent over a thick textbook, pointedly ignoring him.

"That was us, in a nutshell," Natalie said flatly. "Ethan, the tree-hugging dreamer. And me, the only one with a lick of common sense."

Samantha zoomed in on the image, studying the wistful look on young Ethan's face. Reconciling the innocent boy with the man brutally slain in his own fields was difficult.

"I'm afraid I don't have all the details about what happened with your family's farm when your parents could no longer run it, as I wasn't born until well after that. Could you describe the events during that transition period and how old you both were?"

"Our mother, Evelyn Green, died when I was 17 and Ethan was 12. It was extremely difficult for him at that young age. Then our father's tragic accident happened when I was 25 and Ethan was 20 - the same year you were born, 1983. That's when Ethan stepped up to take over running Green Acres."

Sam interjected with a laugh, "Green Acres. For years, I've pondered that moniker, often curious about its origin as the TV show's namesake."

Adjusting her posture, Natalie responded, "Ms. Brewer... Samantha. Our family farm inherited its name from my parents during the 1950s, bearing no relation to that inane television program."

Reddening cheeks accompanied Sam's apology, replying, "Please accept my apology. I meant no disrespect."

She paused, "Anyway, where was I?" Choking back what seemed like a mix of grief and resentment, "I warned him he was too young and idealistic to manage the family business properly. Despite my concerns, he waved them off, determined to convert our traditional crops to his 'sustainable' organic farming methods.

Natalie shook her head, jaw clenched. "It was a disaster from the start. While I was building my career, Ethan just kept sinking more money into that money-pit farm of his."

Her voice rose, drawing curious glances from the other patrons. Natalie took a breath, visibly reining herself in.

"I begged him to see reason - to modernize, expand, treat it like a proper business. But he wouldn't hear of it. He vowed to do things his way, in harmony with Mother Earth.

She uttered the words in a poisonous tone, as if laced with arsenic. "We fought about it for months. Until I finally washed my hands of the whole thing. Of him."

Samantha's pen paused over her notebook. "So you cut off contact with Ethan completely?"

Natalie shrugged, a sharp rise and fall of her shoulders. "What was the point? He made his choice, and I had my life and career to build. I couldn't let his foolishness drag me down."

She sipped her coffee primly. "We exchanged a few letters over the years. Usually when the bank would call about missed payments and I'd have to bail him out. I always made it clear - I wanted nothing to do with that sinking ship he called a farm."

Samantha digested this in silence, her mind whirring. The bitterness and resentment were rolling off Natalie in palpable waves. How deep did that anger truly run?

"Would you be willing to show me those letters?" she asked, keeping her tone strategically neutral. "They could provide valuable insight into Ethan's state of mind leading up to his death."

Natalie's gaze turned flinty. "I'm afraid I don't keep sentimental keepsakes, Miss Brewer. Now, if there's nothing else, I have a busy schedule to attend to."

"I'm also curious, if you don't mind me asking - there were reports of a necklace going missing from the crime scene the night of the murder. An heirloom piece?"

Natalie's expression tightened. "Oh, you're talking about the pearls from my husband? Yes, I mentioned to the police I was wearing them when I went to confront Ethan that night. By the time I got home, they were gone - probably fell off during our argument, though the incompetent police couldn't even find them at the crime scene."

She stood abruptly, the legs of her chair screeching against the hardwood. Samantha scrambled to her feet as well.

"Of course, I understand, but if you could kindly spare a few more minutes - I'd love to see your home, get a sense of your life separate from Ethan's. It would really help construct the profile."

Natalie hesitated, visibly debating the quickest way to be rid of the pesky journalist. Her phone buzzed just then with an incoming text. Natalie checked it and gave an irritated huff.

"Unbelievable. It seems my two o'clock video conference has been postponed until tomorrow because of some supplier issue in Shanghai." She looked up at Samantha, visibly steeling herself. "I suppose that unexpectedly opens up my afternoon."

Natalie set her phone down with a tight smile. "Since I've been inconveniently grounded, I may as well make use of the time. Shall we go over to my home, Miss Brewer? Get... a sense of my life separate from Ethan's, as you put it."

Twenty minutes later, Samantha stood in the cavernous expanse of Natalie's luxury condo. The place was a shrine to modern minimalism - all clean lines and stark whites, with nary a personal touch in sight.

No photos of Ethan, Samantha noted silently, but plenty of frames boasting Natalie's myriad achievements - diplomas, certificates, a "Top 30 Under 30" business award. Above the minimalist fireplace hung an enormous portrait. Natalie posed regally alongside her husband, a striking string of pearls at her throat.

Samantha's gaze lingered on the necklace. "Those pearls..." she began. "Aren't those the ones you said went missing after your argument with Ethan? Your husband's gift?"

Natalie stiffened almost imperceptibly before replying. "Yes, that's them. I should really get a new set one of these days, after that... unpleasantness with Ethan."

Samantha ran a finger over an engraved plaque. "Impressive," Samantha said aloud, stating, "You've certainly made a name for yourself."

"CFO of Sandoval Enterprises," Natalie's voice held a note of pride. "We just completed a major acquisition. The sky's the limit."

She strode into the gleaming chef's kitchen, all stainless steel and granite. Natalie followed Samantha's gaze, her expression unreadable for a moment. Then, almost spontaneously, she said, "Tea? I have a lovely organic white from my last trip to Beijing."

The "o" word hung in the air between them, heavy with irony. Samantha swallowed a knowing smirk. Natalie's eyes briefly flickered with a hint of... something. A fleeting memory of her bond with Ethan? A subtle acknowledgment of her shared history with Samantha?

Samantha blinked, instantly on guard. Was this a ploy to get her to drop her scrutiny? Some misguided attempt to curry favor?

"Please. I'd love some."

As Natalie busied herself with the kettle, Samantha wandered over to the expansive kitchen island. Sleek architecture magazines fanned out across the marble, their covers boasting multi-million dollar homes and über-modern office spaces.

She casually flipped through them, looking for any clue, any scribbled note or circled ad that could hint at a deeper connection to Ethan's world. While they appeared to be just light reading material, the glossy pages remained pristine and unmarked.

Sensing the dead end, Samantha changed tack. She turned to face Natalie head on, her expression open and guileless.

"Dr. Sandoval, I have to ask - given the depths of your estrangement from Ethan, the philosophical differences in your lives... did you ever resent him enough to want him dead?"

Natalie went still, her hand frozen on the whistling kettle. For a moment, Samantha thought she might hurl the scalding water right in her face.

She burst into laughter - a sharp, brittle sound. "Oh, honey. If I bumped off everyone who annoyed me, there'd be bodies piled up down Main Street."

She poured the steaming water into two delicate cups, her movements precise and controlled. "Ethan and I had our differences. I thought he was a fool, tilting at non-GMO windmills. But what would killing him get me? A crumbling farm drowning in debt? Please."

Samantha accepted the tea, breathing in the delicate aroma. She took a sip, considering her next move.

"What if Ethan's debts put your own assets at risk? Your stake in the family property and investments made on behalf of the farm over the years? Surely you'd want to protect what you'd built."

Natalie's cup clattered against the saucer, droplets spattering the granite. "Just what are you implying, Miss Brewer?"

Samantha held up a placating hand. "I'm not implying anything. But I think it's relevant that, by your own admission, Ethan's organic operation was failing. Badly."

She leaned forward, eyes intent. "In fact, I have sources at Willow Creek Savings and Loan who say foreclosure was imminent. The farm was hemorrhaging money, missing payments left and right. It's no secret around town."

A tendon ticked on Natalie's jaw. She looked away, jaw clenched. "No. It wasn't a secret," she ground out. "Ethan refused to face reality, as usual. He just kept sinking more into that money pit, convinced the almighty earthworms would magically turn things around."

Samantha nodded, filing the information away. "And you? With your assets tied to the property, your family name stained by public financial ruin... that must have put you in quite a precarious position. Professionally, personally."

Natalie whirled on her, eyes blazing. "Now you listen here, you two-bit hack! I worked my tail off to achieve my current position. To build something real, something lasting. And I surely didn't let my brother's deluded dream destroy everything I—"

She broke off, chest heaving. In the charged silence, the trilling of Natalie's cell phone sounded like a bomb detonating.

Visibly collecting herself, Natalie grabbed the phone off the counter and glanced at the screen. "It's the office. I have to take this."

She leveled Samantha with an icy glare. "Don't. Touch. Anything."

Then she was gone, her heels clacking thunderously down the hall. Samantha waited half a beat before springing into action.

She darted over to the small desk tucked in the corner, yanking open drawers with abandon. Utility bills, take-out menus, stock prospectuses - she sifted through them quickly, barely breathing.

A red folder caught her eye, the words "Sandoval Enterprises Acquisition" emblazoned across the front in bold print. Heart pounding, Samantha flipped it open, scanning the dense lines of legalese.

There, amidst the endless tangle of legal jargon and convoluted phrasing, a familiar name leapt out at her: Green Acres Farms. Listed as a potential subsidiary target.

Samantha's eyes widened. Why would Natalie be eyeing Ethan's floundering farm as an acquisition? Was she planning some kind of hostile takeover? Angling to push her brother out completely?

Pulse racing, she reached for her phone to snap a covert photo. But before she could swipe to the camera, a shadow fell across the desk.

"Find anything interesting, Miss Brewer?"

Natalie stood rigid in the doorway, her face a mask of cold fury. Samantha straightened slowly, mind spinning for an explanation.

"Dr. Sandoval, I was just—"

"Just violating my privacy and rifling through confidential documents?" Natalie advanced on her, each word precise and devastating. "I knew you were trouble. Should have trusted my gut."

Samantha edged back, hands raised. "I'm just trying to find the truth. For Ethan. Don't you want that?"

"What I want," Natalie hissed, ripping the folder from Samantha's hands, "is for you to get out of my home. Now!"

She gripped Samantha's arm, nails biting into flesh, and forcefully hauled her toward the door.

"If I ever see your duplicitous face again," Natalie snarled, shoving Samantha over the threshold, "you'll be sorting through more legal documents than you can read in a lifetime. I'm talking slander, libel, invasion of privacy - the works."

Then the door slammed with a resounding finality, nearly catching Samantha's nose. She stumbled back, heart galloping against her ribcage.

In a daze, Samantha made her way downstairs and collapsed into her car. She gripped the steering wheel, trying to process what had just happened.

The folder. Green Acres as a target acquisition. It didn't add up - why absorb a failing farm into a thriving corporate structure? Unless Natalie planned to sell off the assets, strip it for parts...

Samantha groaned, thumping her forehead against the steering wheel. Natalie was definitely hiding something, that much was clear. But her explosive reaction—the defensive fury when confronted—hinted at more than just protecting trade secrets.

Rubbing her throbbing temples, Samantha pulled out her phone. Time to call in reinforcements, compare notes with Jenny. She tapped her friend's contact and lifted the phone to her ear, lips pursed as it rang.

And rang. And rang.

Finally going to voicemail, Samantha let out a frustrated sigh and ended the call. Jenny must be knee-deep in her own research. She fired off a quick text: "Call me ASAP. Huge development with Natalie."

Samantha leaned back against the headrest, her head throbbing. She had a sinking feeling they were just scratching the surface of a very deep, very dark well.

Chapter 4

The sun beat down on Samantha's neck as she crunched across the gravel drive of Green Acres Farm, dust billowing in her wake. The sprawling property was a patchwork of lush vegetable fields and wildflower meadows, the very picture of country charm.

But today, the air held a somber weight, the usual birdsong muted in the aftermath of tragedy. Samantha squared her shoulders and pressed on toward the weathered red barn at the far end of the drive.

As she drew closer, the rhythmic clangs and grunts of exertion grew louder. She rounded the corner to find a young man in grease-stained overalls hunched over an ancient tractor, muscled arms straining as he wrestled with a rusted bolt.

"Lucas Fernandez?" Samantha called out, maintaining a respectful distance. No need to spook him right off the bat.

The man startled, whacking his head on the tractor's raised hood. He straightened with a muffled curse, rubbing his close-cropped dark hair.

"Who wants to know?" His voice was guarded, brown eyes narrowed in suspicion.

Samantha offered her most disarming smile. "I'm Samantha Brewer. I'm an old friend and a journalist looking into Ethan Green's death."

She held up her hands in a placating gesture as Lucas tensed. "I'm not here to make accusations. I just want to understand who Ethan was, and hopefully bring his killer to justice."

Lucas studied her suspiciously, wiping his hands on a rag tucked into his back pocket. He was younger than she expected, early 20s at most, with a wiry build and tanned skin that spoke to long hours under the sun.

"Awful convenient, you showing up now," he said, jaw tight. "Where were you when Ethan was alive, huh? When he needed support?"

Samantha felt the jab like a physical blow. He wasn't wrong - she'd been hundreds of miles away, chasing the next big story, while her hometown crumbled. While Ethan fought his battles alone.

She swallowed hard. "I should have been here. I know that. But I'm here now, and I want to help. Ethan was... he was a good man."

Something flickered in Lucas' expression, a chink in the stony facade. He looked away, throat working.

"Yeah. He was."

The words hung between them, heavy with shared grief. After a long moment, Lucas sighed and grabbed a rag to wipe the worst of the grease from his hands.

"Alright, Miss Journalist. You got questions, I got answers. But I gotta keep working while we talk. These tomatoes won't pick themselves."

Samantha fell into step beside him as he stalked off toward the nearest greenhouse, a cavernous plastic structure shimmering with heat.

"So, you worked closely with Ethan?"

"Past three years, ever since I aged out of the system." At Samantha's questioning look, Lucas shrugged. "Foster care. I was what they call a 'troubled youth.' In and out of juvie, bounced around homes. Nobody wanted me."

His voice roughened with old pain. "Until Ethan. He took a chance on me, gave me a job here. Taught me everything I know about organic farming."

Samantha nodded, scribbling in her notebook as they walked. The sun filtering through the plastic cast eerie ripples across the page.

"Seems like you two had a special bond."

A shadow passed over Lucas' face. "I thought so. He wasn't just my boss, he was... he believed in me, you know? Said I had a 'natural touch' with the plants. That I could be a part of something bigger here."

He came to an abrupt stop, and Samantha nearly collided with his back. They'd reached a colorful cluster of beehives, the low thrum of insect activity filling the humid air.

"We built these together," Lucas said, running a hand over the rough-hewn wood. "Part of Ethan's big plan. He wanted this place to be more than just a farm. He had visions of an educational center, where city kids could come and learn about sustainable agriculture."

His voice cracked. "Where kids like me could find purpose, a place to belong."

Samantha's heart clenched. She could vividly picture it - Ethan with his megawatt smile and boundless enthusiasm, sketching out dreams in the rich black soil.

"That sounds amazing," she said softly. Ethan was always a big dreamer.

Lucas huffed a humorless laugh. "Too big for some folks around here."

He set off again at a brisk clip, following a well-worn path through the fragrant herbs and swaying corn stalks. Samantha jogged to keep up.

"The other farmers, you mean? I got the sense Ethan's methods weren't exactly popular with the old guard."

"Understatement of the century." Lucas spat to the side, lip curled. "You know how it is in a place like this. People don't like change. And

Ethan was all about shaking things up, proving that organic could work on a large scale."

He ducked under a low-hanging branch, pollen dusting his dark hair. "Ruffled a lot of feathers with his 'new-age mumbo-jumbo,' as they called it. The herbicide bans, the heirloom seed exchanges. Man, you should've seen their faces when he rolled out the compost partnership with the school district!"

Despite the grim circumstances, Samantha had to bite back a smile at the image. Ethan always loved a good compost heap.

Lucas caught her expression and grinned, a startling flash of white teeth. For a moment, he looked painfully young, unburdened.

Then his face shuttered again. "I just wish…"

He trailed off, shaking his head. Samantha waited, letting the silence stretch as they reached the bubbling creek that cut through the forested edge of the property. Lucas stared into the dappled waters, jaw working.

"You wish what?" Samantha prompted gently.

"I wish I'd had his conviction," Lucas whispered, hands clenching into fists at his sides. "His unshakable belief in what was right. I grew up around conventional farms, you know. Pesticides and GMOs and all that jazz. It's all I knew."

He swallowed hard, Adam's apple bobbing. "And when I first came to work for Ethan, I thought he was nuts. All this talk of sustainability, when I'd grown up seeing farmers use pesticides and RoundUp on crops."

Samantha's grip tightened on her pen. This was the angle she was missing, the key to understanding the tangled web of Ethan's last days.

"So there was tension between you two," she probed, keeping her voice carefully neutral. "A clash of ideologies."

Lucas didn't answer right away. He crouched by the water, cupping his hands to splash his face. The droplets clung to his lashes and stubble, glistening in the mottled sunlight.

"There was," he said roughly, still staring into the ripples. "I resented him, at first. Thought he was just another holier-than-thou environmentalist, telling me my family's way of life was wrong."

He rocked back on his heels, eyes distant. "We fought about it. A lot. Had some real knock-down, drag-out screaming matches in those early days. But Ethan... he never gave up on me."

Lucas' shoulders slumped, his entire body folding in on itself. "Even when I gave him every reason to."

Samantha's heart lodged in her throat. She had a sudden, terrible feeling about where this was headed.

"Lucas," she said quietly, kneeling beside him on the loamy earth. "What happened the night Ethan died?"

A shudder ran through him, a full-body flinch. He squeezed his eyes shut, sucking in a ragged breath.

"We fought," he choked out. "Worse than ever. I... I'd done something real stupid. Sprayed the north field with a pesticide cocktail, the kind Ethan had forbidden on his land."

The words tumbled out of him in a punishing rush. "I don't know what I was thinking. I guess old habits die hard. But when Ethan found out, he just... he lost it. Said I'd betrayed everything he stood for, everything he was trying to teach me."

Lucas pressed the heels of his hands to his eyes, chest heaving. "He said I was just like all the rest. A slave to the poison peddlers, too blind to see I was destroying the very earth that sustained us."

Samantha's stomach churned with sudden, sick understanding. The fight, the illegal spray, the crushing guilt in Lucas' eyes...

Oh, my gosh! Did he actually do it?

"Lucas," she croaked, throat tight. "Are you saying—"

"No!" His head snapped up, wild-eyed. "No, I swear on everything sacred to me, I didn't - I could never..."

He scrambled to his feet, backing away from her like a wounded animal. "I was angry, okay? Hurt and ashamed and so blasted angry, I couldn't see straight. But I didn't kill him!"

His voice cracked on a sob. "I loved him. He was the only person who ever cared about me. I wouldn't... I couldn't..."

Samantha rose, hands raised in supplication. Her heart cracked at the raw anguish twisting his features. "Okay. I believe you."

And she did, with a bone-deep certainty that surprised her. Whatever demons Lucas Fernandez wrestled with, he was no killer. Just a lost soul, drowning in grief and regret.

"I believe you," she repeated softly. "But Lucas, this doesn't look good. The fight, the illegal pesticides... if the Sheriff finds out—"

Lucas blanched, panic flashing in his eyes. "You can't tell him. Please. I'll lose everything, the farm, my future... Ethan's dream..."

Samantha opened her mouth to respond, but was cut off by the insistent trill of her cell phone. She fumbled it out of her pocket, frowning at the unknown number.

"Samantha Brewer."

"Miss Brewer." Sheriff Cooper's gravelly drawl was unmistakable. "We need to talk. Now."

There was a click, and the line went dead. Samantha stared at the phone, an icy trickle of dread between her shoulder blades.

"What is it?" Lucas demanded, voice high and thready. "Was that the cops?"

Samantha slid the phone back into her pocket, mind racing. Whatever this was, it couldn't be good.

"I have to go," she said, fighting to keep her voice level. "But Lucas, listen to me. Don't do anything rash. Let me handle this."

She gripped his shoulder, trying to pour confidence she didn't feel into the touch. "It's going to be okay. I won't let them railroad you."

Lucas searched her face, eyes glassy with unshed tears. He gave a jerky nod. "Okay. Yeah, okay."

Samantha squeezed once, then turned on her heel and hurried back to her car. Her mind spun with possibilities, each more dire than the last.

Sheriff Cooper was waiting in his cramped office, meaty arms folded across his chest. His expression could have curdled milk.

"Sit down, Miss Brewer." It wasn't a request.

Samantha perched on the edge of a hard plastic chair, pulse pounding in her ears. Cooper leaned back, the ancient springs creaking under his bulk.

"Imagine my surprise," he drawled, "when I get a call from Hank Emerson down at the feed store, telling me he spotted you out at Green Acres. Interrogating that Fernandez kid."

Samantha cursed inwardly. Infernal small-town grapevine. "It wasn't an interrogation. We were just talking."

"Uh-huh." Cooper laced his fingers over his straining belt buckle. "Talking. That what you call harassing potential suspects in an ongoing murder investigation?"

Samantha stiffened. "Lucas isn't a suspect."

"Funny, I don't remember asking for your opinion on the matter." The Sheriff's eyes glittered dangerously. "In fact, I don't remember giving you permission to go around poking your nose where it don't belong, period."

Samantha forced herself to take a calming breath. Losing her temper wouldn't help Lucas. Or Ethan.

"You're right," she said evenly. "I overstepped. It won't happen again."

Cooper harrumphed. "Durn tootin' it won't. Because if you keep interfering with my case, I'll slap you with obstruction charges faster 'n a jackrabbit on a hot skillet!"

Samantha clenched her jaw, holding her tongue with Herculean effort. She knew an unwinnable battle when she saw one.

"Understood, Sheriff."

He grunted, apparently satisfied with her capitulation. Then he reached into his desk drawer and pulled out a grainy black-and-white photo.

"Lucky for you, Miss Nancy Drew, turns out the Fernandez kid is in the clear. For now."

Samantha blinked at the image. It was a still from a security camera, time-stamped the night of Ethan's murder. And there, in the fuzzy green haze of night-vision, was the unmistakable figure of Lucas Fernandez.

Slumped over the bar at Rusty's Tavern, a line of shot glasses scattered before him.

"Drowning his sorrows over that little spat with Ethan, looks like," Cooper said, smug satisfaction oozing from every pore. "Got a nice fat time-stamped alibi all night long."

Samantha frowned, scanning the image closer. Something wasn't right. The edges were too crisp, the shadows too deep. It almost looked... altered.

"Sheriff," she drawled, "have you inspected this footage? I suspect someone might have tampered with it."

Cooper's bushy eyebrows shot up. "Excuse me?"

Samantha jabbed a finger at the screen. "Look at these visual artifacts, the blurring here and here. I've seen doctored surveillance video before, and this has all the hallmarks."

The Sheriff snatched the photo back, glowering. "So what, now my evidence is fake? My people don't know how to do their durn jobs?"

"I'm just saying it warrants a closer look—"

"And I'm saying you don't know what in tarnation you're talking about!" Cooper slapped a hand on the desk, jowls quivering with outrage.

Samantha recoiled, eyes wide. She'd struck a nerve, that was clear. But why? What was Cooper trying to hide?

"You listen to me, missy," he growled, jabbing a finger in her direction. "I've been working this beat since you were in diapers. I know how to conduct an investigation, and I sure as blazes don't need some city slicker blogger telling me what evidence is credible."

Samantha opened her mouth to argue, but the thunderous look on Cooper's face made her reconsider. She swallowed hard, pulse pounding in her temples.

"My apologies, Sheriff," she said woodenly. "You're right. I was out of line."

Cooper narrowed his eyes, searching her face for signs of deception. Then he sat back with a huff, the chair groaning in relief.

"Fine. Apology accepted." He waved a dismissive hand. "I'll have my boys take another look at the footage, just to put your overactive imagination at ease. But I'm warning you, Brewer. You step out of line one more time, and I'll make good on my promise."

Obstruction charges. Despite her suspicions about Lucas' doctored alibi footage, he'd put her in a cell right next to him, if he had his way.

Samantha stood on watery legs, her whole body trembling with suppressed rage and frustration. But she pasted on a tight smile, determined not to give Cooper the satisfaction.

"Understood, Sheriff. It won't happen again."

"Make sure it doesn't."

And with that, he dismissed her. Samantha strode from the station, seething. Cooper was hiding something, she was sure of it. And whatever it was, it had the stink of corruption all over it.

As she slid behind the wheel of her car, keyed the ignition and peeled out of the parking lot, tires screeching. Obstruction charges be pushed aside.

Samantha had a sinking feeling about this whole affair. What will she do if the Sheriff is in on this?

Chapter 5

The county fair was in full swing, a riotous explosion of color and sound. Calliope music warred with the shrieks of delighted children as the scents of funnel cake, grilled turkey drumsticks and roasted corn saturated the air.

Samantha Brewer wove through the crowd, her mind a million miles from the festive atmosphere. Thoughts of Ethan's murder case chased themselves in dizzying circles, a tangle of loose threads she couldn't quite unravel.

Lost in contemplation, she collided headfirst with a solid wall of muscle. Strong hands gripped her shoulders, steadying her as a familiar chuckle rumbled above.

"Well, well. Sammie Brewer, as I live and breathe."

Samantha's head snapped up, eyes widening. She knew that voice, that laugh. It had once made her knees weak and her heart race in the halls of Willow Creek High.

"Jake." She breathed his name like a revelation, drinking in the sight of him. Time had been kind to Jake Emerson - his sandy hair was still thick and wavy, his hazel eyes warm as sunbaked earth. Years of farm labor had sculpted the once lanky muscles into something harder.

He smiled down at her, a crooked quirk of the lips that set off a flurry of butterflies in her stomach. Blast that man. Fifteen years later, and he still had the power to reduce her to a blushing schoolgirl.

"It's been a minute, hasn't it?" Jake wrapped her in a hug, the scent of hay and honest sweat enveloping her. "I'm so sorry about Ethan, Sam. I know you two were close."

Samantha returned the embrace briefly before stepping back, composing her features into a mask of professional sympathy.

"Thanks, Jake. It's been a tough few days." She cleared her throat, gesturing vaguely at the fair. "I'm surprised to see you here, to be honest. Figured you'd be out in the fields, what with harvest season coming up."

Jake shrugged, his grin turning rueful. "What can I say? Even us country boys require occasional breaks. Besides, I promised Heather I'd win her the biggest teddy bear in the ring toss."

Heather. Of course. Samantha mentally kicked herself for the little flip of disappointment in her belly. She'd forgotten Jake was engaged, set to marry his local sweetheart in a few short months.

She pasted on a bright smile. "That's great, Jake. I'm thrilled for you two." The words tasted like sawdust on her tongue.

An awkward silence descended, thick with unspoken history. Jake rubbed the back of his neck, a nervous tell Samantha recognized from their fumbling teenage encounters.

"Listen, Sam... I heard you're looking into Ethan's death. Trying to figure out what really happened." His voice dropped, brow furrowing. "I'm here to help you in any way possible."

Samantha's spine stiffened, her investigative instincts sparking to life. This was it. The opening she needed to probe Jake's knowledge of the case, his potential involvement.

She linked her arm through his, steering him toward the picnic area. "Actually, I would love to pick your brain if you've got a minute. Walk with me?"

Jake hesitated for the barest fraction of a second before nodding, allowing himself to be led. They strolled past the midway, the flashing lights and tinny music fading into the background.

Samantha kept her tone light, conversational. "So, how's life been treating you, Farmer Emerson? I see the family business is still going strong."

Jake chuckled, but there was an undercurrent of strain beneath the sound. "Oh, you know how it is. Up at dawn, asleep by dusk. Watching the sky and praying for rain. Rinse and repeat."

He kicked at a stray pebble, hands shoved deep in his pockets. "It's a good life, don't get me wrong. Honest work, fresh air. But sometimes..."

He trailed off, shaking his head. Samantha waited, the silence stretching taut between them.

"Sometimes I wonder if it's all worth it, you know?" Jake's voice was soft, almost lost beneath the distant carousel music. "The long hours, the backbreaking labor. The constant battle against drought and blight and every other doggone thing Mother Nature can throw at you."

Samantha made an indistinct sound of sympathy. "It's not a simple path you've chosen. I can't imagine the grit it takes to pour your blood and sweat into the land like that."

Jake huffed a bitter laugh. "You want to know the real kicker? It still isn't enough. Not for some folks, anyway."

There was an edge to his words, sharp as a scythe. Samantha's pulse quickened. They were getting somewhere now.

She kept her expression cautiously neutral. "Folks like Ethan, you mean?"

Jake's head whipped around, hazel eyes narrowing. "Now, what's that supposed to mean?"

Samantha held up a placating hand. "I just meant, it's no secret there was bad blood between the Emersons and the Greens. Especially with farming practices."

She let the statement hang, an unspoken question. Jake worked his jaw, the muscles bunching and flexing beneath tanned skin.

For a long moment, Samantha thought he might withdraw, retreat behind the simple charm and aw-shucks smiles. But then his shoulders slumped, the fight draining out of him like water from a cracked vessel.

"Ethan was... he was a good man. Principled. Passionate." Jake shook his head, a wry twist to his mouth. "But man, he was incredibly stubborn. Once he got an idea in his head, he became immovable. No matter how much it might cost him."

Samantha leaned forward, sensing the cracks in Jake's armor. "Cost him how?"

Jake blew out a breath, raking a hand through his hair. "You remember the town hall meeting... must've been about five years back? When Ethan tried to push through that resolution, banning all synthetic pesticides and herbicides in the county?"

Samantha nodded slowly, memory stirring. It had been a contentious issue, dividing the town along stark lines - the organic devotees versus the conventional old guard. Ethan had been the face of the former, a vocal crusader for his chemical-free cause.

"I remember. Things got pretty heated, as I recall."

Jake barked a mirthless laugh. "Heated? Sam, it was a full-on war. My dad and Ethan went at each other like a pair of junkyard dogs. Hollering and red-faced, veins popping, the whole nine."

He shook his head, eyes distant with the memory. "I was certain they would fight, right there in front of God and the town council. And all over some blasted bug spray."

Samantha's mind raced, the puzzle pieces clicking into place. Ethan's crusade against agribusiness. Jake's family's entrenched resistance. The simmering resentments and philosophical rifts, boiling over into open hostility.

It was a powder keg, primed and ready to blow. And Ethan's murder was the match that lit the fuse.

She kept her voice carefully measured, not wanting to spook Jake. "That must have been hard for you. Being caught in the middle like that, between your family and your friend."

Jake's laugh held no humor. "Friend. Right." He scrubbed a hand over his face, his 30-odd years becoming apparent in an instant.

"Truth is, Ethan and I... we weren't really friends. Not for a long time. Not since he started getting all high and mighty about his organic shtick, acting like the rest of us were poisoning the earth and ruining lives with our 'conventional' ways."

The bitterness rose off him in waves, palpable and choking. Samantha swallowed hard against the sudden lump in her throat.

"Jake..." She reached out, laying a tentative hand on his arm. He flinched but didn't pull away. "I have to ask. Where were you, the morning Ethan died?"

He stiffened, the muscles bunching beneath her fingers. For a second, Samantha thought he might bolt. But then he sagged, the fight draining out of him.

"I was in the north fields. Harvesting potatoes." His voice was flat, routine. Like he'd rehearsed the words a thousand times. "Alone. Like every morning for the past decade."

Samantha's heart sank. It was the same story he'd told the Sheriff, the same flimsy alibi. But something in his demeanor, the dullness of his eyes, made her wonder.

Was it the truth? Or a well-worn lie, polished smooth with repetition?

She opened her mouth to press further, but a piercing squeal of delight interrupted her. A blonde woman was bounding toward them, a giant teddy bear clutched in her arms.

"Babe! I can't believe you actually won it!" The woman - Heather, Samantha presumed - launched herself at Jake, nearly bowling him over with the force of her hug.

Jake's face split into a grin, the shadows banished in an instant. He swung Heather around, planting a smacking kiss on her lips.

"Told you I'd get it, didn't I? Nothing but the best for my girl."

Heather giggled, swatting at his chest. Then her gaze landed on Samantha, and her smile faltered.

"Oh. Hello," she said politely, but her eyes showed a hint of wariness. A woman assessing competition.

Samantha pasted on her best harmless smile. "Hi there. I'm Samantha Brewer, an old friend of Jake's. I was just passing through town and thought I'd say hello."

Heather's answering smile was tight. "Of course. Jake's mentioned you." The unspoken 'once or twice in passing' hung in the air.

Heather had been a few years behind us at Willow Creek High, but she surely remembers me - Jake's ex from high school—now resurfacing after all these years.

An awkward beat, then Jake cleared his throat. "Well, uh, we should probably get going. The tractor pull is starting soon, and we have to get close seats."

He shot Samantha an apologetic look. "Good to see you, Sam. And hey, try not to worry too much about all this murder business, okay? I'm sure the Sheriff will unravel it."

With one last brusque hug, he allowed Heather to lead him away, the teddy bear bobbing forlornly between them. Samantha watched them go, a sour taste in her mouth.

Try not to worry. Easy for him to say. He wasn't the one who had lost a close friend, with the killer still free.

Samantha shook herself, tucking away the unwelcome flutter of jealousy. She had work to do.

The Emerson farm was quiet, the fields stretching out in orderly rows. Samantha parked her car at the end of the long dirt drive, slipping out into the honeyed afternoon light.

She kept to the edges of the property, not wanting to draw attention. The big red barn loomed ahead, its weathered wood warm and inviting in the sun.

Sam, what are you doing here? This is crazy. She repositioned herself along the fence and could see an enormous machine shed attached to the barn. I wonder...

Samantha darted a quick glance around, then slipped inside, easing the door shut behind her. The thick smell of straw and manure enveloped her undercut with the faint metallic tang of motor oil.

She moved deeper into the cavernous space, eyes straining in the gloom. Hulking shapes of farm equipment lurked in the shadows, silent and waiting.

What was she even looking for? Some kind of smoking gun, a clue that would tie Jake to Ethan's murder? It was a long shot, and she knew it.

But she had to try. For Ethan's sake. For her own peace of mind.

Samantha was elbow-deep in a rustling pile of hay, praying she didn't encounter any snakes, when a voice rang out behind her.

"Hey! What do you think you're doing?"

She whirled, heart in her throat. A burly man in overalls was standing in the doorway, pitchfork clutched in his beefy hands.

Samantha stammered, mind racing for an excuse. "I was just..."

"Just snooping around where you don't belong?" The man advanced, his face a thundercloud. "You're trespassing, Miss Muffet. I suggest you get off this property before I call the sheriff's station."

Samantha's stomach bottomed out. The last thing she needed was another run-in with Sheriff Cooper, especially after their last contentious encounter.

She held up her hands in surrender, backing toward the door. "Okay, okay. I'm going. No need to get worked up."

The farmhand glowered, the pitchfork steady in his hands. "I mean it. If I see you around here again, there will be trouble. Understand?"

Samantha nodded vigorously, not trusting her voice. She stumbled out the door, into the blinding sunlight.

She made it back to her car in record time, pulse pounding in her ears. With shaking hands, she keyed the ignition, gravel spraying as she peeled out onto the road.

What was she thinking, skulking around the Emerson farm like some amateur sleuth? She was going to get herself arrested. Or worse.

Samantha thumped the steering wheel in frustration. She'd let her history with Jake cloud her judgment, allowed those lingering teenage feelings to override her common sense.

It was a rookie mistake. One she couldn't afford to make again.

By the time she pulled up to Delores' house, Samantha had composed herself. She pasted on a bright smile as her mother opened the door, praying it didn't look as manic as it felt.

"Samantha, dear! I was worrying." Delores ushered her inside, fussing and clucking. "You missed supper. I had to put the roast in the fridge."

"Sorry, Mom. I got caught up with... work stuff." Samantha hedged, shrugging out of her jacket. She dreaded another lecture about staying out of the investigation.

Delores peered at her over the rims of her bifocals. "Work stuff. I see." Her tone was bland, but her eyes were sharp. "And I suppose this 'work stuff' had nothing to do with you traipsing around town with Jake Emerson?"

Samantha's stomach lurched. Blast it all, Willow Creek and its lightning-fast gossip mill.

"It's not what you think," she began, but Delores cut her off with a wave.

"Oh, spare me the denials, Samantha. I know that look."

Samantha flushed, heat crawling up her neck. "Mom, really. There's nothing going on with me and Jake. I was just... following a lead."

Delores harrumphed, clearly unconvinced. "A lead. Is that what they're calling it these days?"

She softened, patting Samantha's cheek. "Just be careful, dear. I know young love can exhilarate, but you have a bright future ahead of you. Don't let old flames burn you up."

With that cryptic warning, she tottered off to bed, leaving Samantha alone with her churning thoughts.

Sleep was a struggle that night. Samantha tossed and turned, her mind a whirl of memory and suspicion.

Jake's face swam behind her eyelids, that crooked grin making her heart clench. But then it morphed, hardening into something cold and unrecognizable. Something that could plunge a knife into Ethan's chest and walk away.

No. Samantha rolled over, punching her pillow. She couldn't think like that. Jake was many things - impulsive, hotheaded, even a little pig-headed. But he wasn't a killer.

Was he?

Her cell phone trilled, jolting her out of her dark reverie. Samantha fumbled for it, squinting at the display. The screen blinked, "Unknown Caller."

A tendril of unease wormed its way through her gut as she lifted the phone to her ear. "Hello?"

"Miss Brewer?" The gruff voice sounded familiar. "Sergeant Patterson from the sheriff's office. Sorry for the late hour, but the Sheriff requires your presence at the station right away."

Samantha sat up straighter, sheets pooling around her waist. "What's this about? Has something happened?"

"Wouldn't say if I knew," the sergeant replied flatly. "Just said it's about that Jake Emerson fella and some new anonymous tip about his involvement in the Ethan Green murder."

The line went dead with an abrupt click. Samantha stared at the silent phone, her heart jackhammering.

Something didn't feel right. Cooper knew it was not the right time to summon her at this hour over a tip. She punched in the sheriff's office number with shaking fingers.

"Willow Creek Sheriff's Department," a bored voice answered.

"Yes, hi, I just received a call from Sergeant Patterson saying I needed to come down to the station immediately to see the Sheriff. About Jake Emerson?"

There was a pause, the sound of shuffling papers. "That's weird, ma'am. There's no Sergeant Patterson that works here and Sheriff Cooper left hours ago. He ain't even here right now."

The hair prickled on the back of Samantha's neck. "I see. Thank you." She ended the call, bile rising in her throat.

Either this was an ill-timed prank, or someone was going to great lengths to rattle her focus on Jake's potential involvement. But who? And why?

Trapped in a maze of deception, Samantha felt her grip on the investigation slipping through her fingers.

It looked like her troubles were just beginning. She wondered what trap waited for her if she went to the station right now... She pondered again the possibility of the Sheriff's involvement.

Chapter 6

The Willow Creek Community Church potluck was in full swing, a sea of pastel polyester and Pyrex dishes. Samantha Brewer weaved through the chattering throng, her paper plate sagging under the weight of Delores Brewer's famous baked ziti.

She spotted her mother holding court at a corner table, surrounded by a gaggle of blue-haired cronies. Delores caught her eye and waved her over, her smile bright as the costume jewelry jangling at her wrists.

"Samantha, dear! Come sit with us." Delores patted the empty chair beside her. "Ladies, you all remember my daughter, the big city journalist."

A chorus of cooing and clucking rose from the assembled women. Samantha pasted on a smile, steeling herself for the onslaught.

"Of course we remember little Sammie," trilled Ms. Cramer, the librarian. "Though I daresay she's not so little anymore!"

"And quite the accomplished young lady, from what I hear," added Mrs. Applebaum, her first grade teacher. Her rheumy eyes gleamed with avid curiosity. "Solving murders and whatnot."

Samantha sank into her seat, cheeks warming under the collective scrutiny. She should have known Delores would waste no time in parading her like a prized pony.

"I wouldn't say solving, exactly," she demurred, poking at her ziti. "I'm only... looking into a few things. Trying to understand what happened to Ethan."

The mere mention of Ethan's name set off a flurry of tongue-clucking and head-shaking. Delores leaned in, eyes wide with feigned shock.

"Oh, it's just too awful for words," she declared, one hand fluttering to her ample bosom. "That poor, misguided boy. What a terrible way to go!"

"I heard," Ms. Cramer said in a stage whisper, "he got involved with that new-age woman. You know, the one with all the crystals and the organic soap stand at the Farmer's Market?"

"Liza Peltier," supplied Mrs. Applebaum, nodding sagely. "Flighty thing always talking about auras and energy fields. Not surprised she'd get tangled up in something unsavory."

Samantha's ears pricked. Liza Peltier. The name was vaguely familiar, but she couldn't quite place it. She made a mental note to follow up on that lead.

"In fact," Ms. Cramer continued, eyes darting around conspiratorially, "I saw her myself leaving Ethan's farm the night before they found the body. Looked mighty upset, too. Tears and everything."

The ladies made appropriately scandalized noises. Samantha leaned forward, journalistic instincts sparking to life.

"What time was this, Ms. Cramer? Did you see which direction she went?"

The librarian blinked, taken aback by the sudden intensity of Samantha's gaze. "Well, I... it was late, mind you. Around ten o'clock, I'd say. I was driving home from my shift at the library, and I saw her tearing out of there in that beat-up VW bus of hers. Headed west, toward the highway."

Samantha jotted the information down on a napkin, mind whirring. West. Toward the Peltier farm, if she remembered correctly. Interesting.

Mrs. Applebaum cleared her throat, eager to contribute her own tidbit. "Of course, Liza's not the only one Ethan was feuding with. There was that whole kerfuffle with Harold Westin and the bees."

Samantha glanced up from her impromptu notes. "Harold Westin? The retired widower who lives out by the quarry?"

Delores sniffed. "That's the one. Odd duck, that Harold. Keeps to himself mostly, ever since his wife passed. He and Ethan had a recent argument. Something about a colony of bees that settled on the border of their properties."

Mrs. Applebaum nodded vigorously, her perm bobbing. "I heard it from Margie down at the post office. Apparently, Harold was fit to be tied over those bees. Said they were terrorizing his prize tomatoes, or some such nonsense."

Ms. Cramer leaned in, eyes gleaming. "And then, bold as brass, he marches up to Ethan in the middle of the feed store and starts ranting and raving. Saying he's going to take matters into his own hands if Ethan doesn't handle the bees."

A frisson of unease prickled down Samantha's spine. "Take matters into his own hands? That sounds... ominous."

Delores waved a dismissive hand. "Oh, you know how men are. All bluster and bravado. I'm sure Harold meant nothing by it. He wouldn't hurt a fly."

Samantha wasn't so sure. In her experience, even the most seemingly harmless individuals could commit dark deeds under the right circumstances. And Harold Westin had just rocketed to the top of her suspect list.

She turned to Delores, fixing her with a probing stare. "What do you think, Mom? Among the people Ethan disagreed with... who do you think had the strongest motive?"

Delores fluttered her lashes, the picture of shocked innocence. "Me? Oh, I couldn't possibly speculate. You know I don't like to make rash judgments in such delicate matters."

Samantha barely refrained from rolling her eyes. Delores Brewer's specialty was making rash judgments. The woman thrived on gossip and innuendo like a plant on sunshine.

But she simply nodded, playing along. "Of course, Mom. I wouldn't want to embarrass you."

The conversation shifted to more mundane matters - Mrs. Applebaum's bunions, Ms. Cramer's ongoing feud with the library's finicky copier. Samantha made her excuses and slipped away, mind churning with the new information.

She was so preoccupied, she almost missed Delores pressing something into her hand as they left the church. It was a newspaper clipping, yellowed and brittle with age.

"Thought this might be of interest," Delores murmured, eyes gleaming with smug intelligence. "Given your current investigation and all."

Samantha scanned the headline, pulse quickening. "Local Farmer Protests Biotech Plans at Agricultural College." The accompanying photo showed Ethan, face set in righteous determination, holding a hand-painted sign outside the stately brick buildings of Willow Creek University.

She looked up at Delores, brow furrowed. "This is from last year. What's its connection to Ethan's murder?"

Delores smiled, tight-lipped. "Oh, I'm sure I don't know. But it seems our dear departed Ethan had quite a knack for making enemies in high places. Might be worth considering, is all I'm saying."

An insistent mental kick jolted Samantha's investigative instincts. Of course, the article about Ethan's protests against the university was relevant - it highlighted potential bad blood with powerful people who could have wanted him silenced. What was I thinking? As an experienced investigator, I should have put it together immediately instead of needing my mother's not-so-subtle prodding.

With that cryptic pronouncement, she flounced off to shake hands with Pastor Mike, leaving Samantha staring after her in consternation.

Later, ensconced in Delores' frilly guest room, Samantha pored over the clipping. According to the article, Ethan had been a vocal opponent of the agriculture department's plans to partner with BiovocaX, a major biotech corporation. He claimed their genetically engineered seed products were harmful to the environment and a threat to small family farms like his own.

The protests had garnered significant media attention and no small amount of backlash from the university. Samantha pondered as she chewed her pen. Could one of Ethan's academic adversaries have taken their disagreement to a murderous extreme?

A knock at the door startled her out of her musings. Delores poked her head in, bearing a tray of tea and cookies.

"Are you staying up late working again?" Delores clucked, setting down the tea tray. "Any fun tidbits to share with your dear old mother?"

Samantha suppressed an eye-roll. "You know I can't discuss the details of an ongoing investigation, Mom."

"Of course, of course." Delores waved a hand airily before fixing Samantha with a serious look. "But that's precisely why I'm... concerned, dear."

She leaned in, voice lowering conspiratorially. "Word's getting around town about your methods. Asking too many probing questions, sticking that nose where it doesn't belong."

Samantha stilled, the hairs prickling on her nape. "What are you talking about?"

"I'm just the messenger!" Delores held up placating hands. "But there are rumblings that certain folks aren't too thrilled with your... zeal for the truth, let's call it. Whispers that you might stir up a hornet's nest, poking around in business that doesn't concern you."

There was an undercurrent of steel beneath the saccharine tone, a subtle edge that made the nebulous warnings land with more weight.

"Who exactly is saying these things?" Samantha fought to keep her voice level. "The Sheriff?"

Delores made a show of zipping her lips. "A lady never reveals her sources, dear. Let's just say... there are certain parties involved in this whole sordid affair who prefer their secrets stayed buried, if you catch my meaning."

The chill that snaked down Samantha's spine was impossible to suppress. Her mother's nonchalant gossip had taken on a distinctly ominous tenor, hinting at darker currents lurking beneath the surface.

"I'm just trying to find the truth, Mom," she said carefully. "Whoever's uncomfortable with that isn't really my concern."

Delores held up a staying hand. "I pray you're right, Samantha. For your sake, I truly do. This town can have... a long memory with indiscretions. Best to let sleeping dogs lie, hmm?"

With that final cryptic caution, she rose and padded towards the door, leaving a cloying trail of metaphorical breadcrumbs in her wake, leaving Samantha to stew in a mix of disbelief and simmering anger.

Samantha sighed, pinching the bridge of her nose as a wave of irritation washed over her. As maddening as her mother's obfuscation could be, she knew Delores' roundabout warnings stemmed from a misguided place of concern. In her own ham-fisted way, she was trying to protect Samantha from potential blowback over her investigation.

Delores had no right to dictate what truths could be revealed. Samantha was a professional, not some gossip-peddling scandal rag. If only her mother would be honest about her fears, perhaps they could...

Delores vanished down the hall, and the thought faded. Samantha's jaw tightened, her gut roiling with a potent mix of affection and frustration for the meddlesome woman. Uncovering Ethan's killer was too important to be deterred by vague threats, no matter how well-intentioned. She'd pursue the truth, come what may. It's what Ethan would have wanted.

Chapter 7

Dust motes swirled in the watery light filtering through the Willow Creek Public Library's grimy windows. Samantha Brewer hunched over the microfiche reader, scrolling through yellowed newspaper archives with single-minded intensity.

The clacking of sensible shoes on linoleum alerted her to an unwanted presence. Ms. Cramer, the stern-faced librarian, loomed over Samantha's shoulder like a tweed-clad gargoyle.

"Finding everything alright, dear?" Her voice was sugary, but her eyes glinted with suspicion behind horn-rimmed glasses. "You've been at it for hours."

Samantha resisted the urge to block the screen with her body. She pasted on a bland smile. "Just doing some research for a project. You know how it is."

Ms. Cramer made a noncommittal noise, craning her neck to get a better look. Samantha casually shifted, angling her notepad out of view. The last thing she needed was the town gossip getting wind of her investigation.

"Well, holler if you need anything." Ms. Cramer finally retreated, disappointment etched in the lines around her mouth.

Samantha breathed a sigh of relief and turned back to the screen. She'd hit the jackpot with these archives - article after article detailing Ethan Green's activist history, his passionate crusade against the agribusiness giants.

Reports of protests erupted outside Willow Creek Agricultural College, where the biotech labs produced genetically engineered crops. Quotes from Ethan, fiery and uncompromising, denouncing the "poison peddlers" and their "Frankenfoods."

And lists of his enemies, long and powerful. Monsanto. DuPont. Syngenta. All with deep pockets and even deeper ties to the college's research programs.

Samantha's pen flew across the page, connecting the dots. For years, Ethan challenged Big Ag, a lone voice of dissent in a town devoted to industrialized farming. To what extent would they silence him?

Heart pounding, she gathered up her notes and headed for the door. She had a hunch, and she needed to follow it. Now.

Samantha burst through the library's double doors, clutching her notebook to her chest. The stale, book-laden air gave way to the crisp autumn chill of late afternoon.

Her well-worn boots crunched over scattered leaves as she made a beeline for her mud-spattered Honda Civic parked at the far end of the lot. Her mind raced, piecing together the disturbing picture emerging from those archived articles.

Ethan had poked a furious bear - no, an entire den of them. The more she learned about his environmental activism, the more Samantha realized how many powerful entities had a motive to want him silenced.

She dug her keys out of her jacket pocket, fingers numb from the cold metal. As she neared the Honda, she slowed, something that struck her as off. Samantha squinted, peering closer.

All four tires were flat, sitting uselessly against the asphalt like deflated balloons.

An expletive burst from her lips as she took in the damage. Someone doesn't like me.

Samantha crouched down, examining the jagged punctures in the sidewalls. It was obvious this was no accident - someone had intentionally ruined her tires.

Her pulse quickened as her gaze darted around the deserted parking lot. Was this a random act of vandalism, or a pointed warning for her to back off her investigation?

Straightening up, she scanned the surrounding area, searching for any sign of her assailant. The only movement came from a stray plastic bag skittering across the pavement, propelled by the brisk wind.

Samantha chewed her lip, debating her next move. She needed to get out of this exposed position, find somewhere secure to regroup. Calling the cops would only slow her down and invite more questions than answers.

She fished out her phone, first calling a tow truck from Bucky's Auto Repair to haul away her disabled Honda. After arranging that, she pulled up Jenny Mack's number at the Willow Creek Chronicle.

"Jen, hey, it's Sam. Listen, I'm in a bit of a jam..." She quickly revealed the situation with her slashed tires.

"No problem, girl, I've got you covered," Jenny's warm voice crackled over the line. "I have a spare junker I can loan you until you get yours fixed up."

Relief washed over Samantha. "You're a lifesaver, Jen. I owe you one."

Forty-five minutes later, she was rolling up to the Willow Creek Agricultural College campus in Jenny's beat-up Ford Taurus, resolve burning bright. The Willow Creek Agricultural College campus was a sprawling monstrosity of brutalist architecture and manicured lawns.

Samantha parked across from the research building, a hulking concrete slab that squatted like a toad among the ivy-covered halls.

She pulled out her phone and snapped a few quick photos, zooming in on the security cameras that bristled from every corner.

Getting inside would be tricky, but not impossible. Not for a resourceful reporter with resources.

Samantha was still strategizing when the crackle of a police radio made her jump. Sheriff Cooper's cruiser rolled up beside her, the man himself glowering from behind the wheel.

"Miss Brewer." His voice was flat, unamused. "Fancy meeting you here. Planning a little breaking and entering, are we?"

Samantha schooled her features into wide-eyed innocence. "Of course not, Sheriff. I was just admiring the... architecture."

Cooper snorted. "Sure you were. And I'm the Queen of Sheba." He leaned across the passenger seat, fixing her with a gimlet eye.

"Listen up, Nancy Drew. I know you've got it in your head to play detective on this case. But I'm only gonna say this once: leave the investigating to the professionals. If you meddle in police business, I'll have you in cuffs faster than a spooked chicken in a coop. We clear?"

Samantha gritted her teeth, fingers tightening on the steering wheel. The urge to tell Cooper precisely what he could do with his condescending advice was overwhelming. But she needed to play nice, at least for now.

"Crystal, Sheriff. I wouldn't dream of interfering." The lie tasted bitter on her tongue.

Cooper grunted, unconvinced. "See that you don't. I've got my eye on you, missy."

With that ominous proclamation, he peeled away, leaving Samantha seething in a cloud of exhaust. Interfering her left foot. She was trying to solve a murder, for Pete's sake!

But Cooper's warning had spooked her. She couldn't afford to get caught snooping if she wished to continue investigating. She needed to be smarter, stealthier.

Which was how she found herself, hours later, skulking around the police impound lot in head-to-toe black, lock picks in hand.

The night was moonless, the air thick with the stench of motor oil and stale cigarettes. Samantha crept through the rows of wrecked cars, heart hammering against her ribs.

There. Ethan's battered pickup, its green paint barely visible under the spatter of mud and crime scene tape. Samantha made quick work of the padlock, wincing at the screech of rusted metal.

She hoisted herself into the cab, wrinkling her nose at the cloying scent of spoiled produce. Ethan had been hauling a load of organic vegetables when he died, the crates now moldering in the summer heat.

Undeterred, Samantha dug through the glove box, the center console, under the seats. She sought anything out of the ordinary, any clue that might point to Ethan's killer.

She was elbow-deep in a pile of fast food wrappers when her fingers brushed against something smooth and plastic. A bag tucked behind the passenger seat.

Heart in her throat, Samantha tugged it free. The object weighed heavily, containing a gritty powder. She held it up to the faint light filtering through the windshield, squinting to read the label.

Ammonium nitrate fertilizer. The same stuff used in homemade bombs.

Samantha's blood ran cold. What on earth was Ethan doing with this? She fumbled for her phone, snapping pictures with shaking hands.

The crunch of gravel made her freeze, pulse spiking. Footsteps drawing closer. The steady sweep of a flashlight beam.

Great! A security guard, making his rounds.

Samantha shoved the bag back where she found it and frantically scanned for an escape route. But the footsteps neared, the light stabbing through the truck's windows.

No choice. She flung herself down, burrowing under the clutter of tarps and feed sacks. With bated breath, she watched as the beam of light danced over the dashboard, inches from her face.

An eternity passed. Then, mercifully, the footsteps receded, the light winking out. Samantha counted to one hundred before she dared to move, every muscle screaming in protest.

She tumbled out of the truck, her knees trembling with spent adrenaline. Empty-handed, but not empty-headed. The photos on her phone were worth more than gold - a lead, at last.

Now she had to decipher its significance. And stay one step ahead of the Sheriff while she did it.

The next morning found Samantha groggy and irritable, mainlining coffee at Mae's Diner. She poked a rubbery egg, mind churning over the events of the previous night.

The bell above the door jingled, and Samantha raised her head, only to grimace. Sheriff Cooper was bearing down on her like a thunderhead, jaw clenched and eyes blazing.

"Well, well. If it isn't Little Miss Breaking and Entering." He loomed over her booth, hands on his utility belt. "Have a fun night, did we?"

Samantha's stomach dropped. He knew. Of course, he knew. She fought to keep her expression neutral, mind racing for an alibi.

"I don't know what you're talking about, Sheriff. I was home all night, sleeping like a baby."

Cooper howled a mirthless laugh. "Sure you were. And I suppose that's not your dirty little paw prints all over Ethan Green's truck?"

He leaned in, voice dropping to a menacing whisper. "I warned you, Brewer. I told you to keep your nose out of police business. But you just couldn't help yourself, could you? Had to go sticking it where it don't belong."

Samantha bristled, anger overpowering self-preservation for a moment. "I'm trying to find the truth, Sheriff. Something you and your boys seem to have trouble with."

Cooper's face turned an alarming shade of purple. "The truth? You wouldn't know the truth if it bit you on your rear end! You're just a nosy little girl playing at being a reporter, stirring up trouble where there ain't none."

He jabbed a finger in her face, close enough to smell the Aqua Velva on his face. "Now you listen, and you listen good. You pull another stunt like that, and I'll have you locked up quicker than a startled deer high-tailin' it through the woods. Interfering with a police investigation is a serious offense, missy. One that comes with real consequences."

Samantha swallowed hard, the reality of her situation sinking in like a stone. Cooper had her dead to rights. If he wanted to, he could make her life a living nightmare - or worse, derail the investigation entirely.

She needed to regroup and find a new approach. One that didn't involve trespassing and petty larceny.

"Alright, Sheriff. You've made your point." She held up her hands in surrender, hating the tremble in her voice. "It won't happen again."

Cooper straightened, smug satisfaction oozing from every pore. "See that it don't. I'll be watching you, Brewer. Like a hawk."

He turned on his heel and stalked out, leaving Samantha to marinate in a mix of frustration and impotent rage. She couldn't let Cooper bully her into submission. Ethan deserved better than that.

But she couldn't be stupid about it either. She needed to play this smart, stay under the radar. And she knew just where to start.

Harold Westin's house was a ramshackle affair on the outskirts of town, surrounded by a wild tangle of honeysuckle and kudzu. Samantha watched from her car as the old man puttered in his garden, oblivious to her presence.

She'd been tailing him for hours, ever since she'd spotted him coming out of the feed store with an armload of unmarked bags. Bags that looked an awful lot like the one she'd found in Ethan's truck.

Harold straightened, wiping his brow with a bandana. Then he headed for his battered Chevy pickup, tossing the bags in the bed with a furtive glance over his shoulder.

Bingo. Samantha waited until he'd pulled out of the driveway before easing out behind him, keeping a discreet distance. She had a hunch Harold wasn't just heading out for a Sunday drive.

Her suspicions were confirmed when he turned onto the highway, heading toward the agricultural college. Samantha's pulse quickened. The pieces were falling into place, a picture beginning to emerge.

But what was it? A picture of an old man with a grudge, caught up in something bigger than himself? Or a killer, cool and calculating, tying up loose ends?

She tailed him to the research building, watching from a distance as he unloaded the bags and disappeared inside. Her fingers itched to follow, to confront him and demand answers.

But Cooper's warning echoed in her ears, a splash of cold water on her eagerness. She couldn't afford another reckless move. Not now, when she was so close.

Chewing her lip in frustration, Samantha contented herself with snapping photos of Harold's license plate, of the unmarked bags sitting on the loading dock. It wasn't much, but it was something. Another breadcrumb on the trail.

The chirp of her phone made her jump, a jolt of fear lancing through her chest. An unknown number, the ID blocked.

"Hello?" She winced at the tremor in her voice.

"Stop digging." Some kind of modulator, low and distorted, masked the voice. "You're in over your head, little girl. Drop it now, while you still can."

Samantha's mouth went dry, a cold sweat breaking out on her temples. "Who is this? What do you want?"

"Consider this a friendly warning. Keep sticking your nose where it doesn't belong, and you might just lose it."

Click. Dial tone.

Samantha stared at the phone, numb with shock. Someone was watching her. Someone who didn't want Ethan's murder solved.

She thought of the leads she'd chased, the secrets she'd uncovered. The resentment in Natalie's eyes, the guilt in Lucas'. The bitter feud between Harold and Ethan, the dark money funding the college's biotech research.

Any of them could be the killer. Any one of them could be on the other end of that phone, a shadowy figure pulling strings, desperate to hide the truth.

The thought made her stomach turn, a sour taste flooding her mouth. But beneath the fear, a small, stubborn ember kindled to life.

They wanted her to be afraid. They wanted her to give up, to slink away like a whipped dog.

Well, forget that noise. Samantha Brewer was no coward. And she sure as shootin' wouldn't let some anonymous goon scare her off the trail.

But she couldn't do it alone. Not anymore. She needed help, needed someone she could trust to watch her back.

She scrolled through her contacts, thumb hovering over Jake's name. A complicated choice, fraught with history and unresolved feelings.

Ultimately, no choice at all. Jake was solid, dependable. A port in the storm. If anyone could help her navigate these treacherous waters, he could.

Samantha hit the call button, heart in her throat as it rang once, twice. On the third ring, Jake's warm baritone filled her ear, nostalgically familiar.

"Sam? What's up?"

"Hey. Can you meet me? I need to talk to you. It's important."

A pause, heavy with unspoken questions. Then, "Sure. Give me twenty."

Samantha sagged in relief, the knot in her chest loosening a fraction. "Thanks, Jake. I owe you one."

"You don't owe me anything, Sam. I'm just glad you called. Where do you want to meet?"

Samantha opened her mouth to respond, but her gaze snagged on a familiar figure emerging from the research building across the way. Harold Westin, that satisfied grin etched on his weathered face.

A new plan formulated in an instant. "Actually, I'll have to get back to you on that meeting. Something that has come up that I need to address first."

"Okay. Just let me know."

She struggled to express her apologies and explanations, feeling overwhelmed. But they could wait. Right now, she needed to solve a murder.

She pocketed the phone and started the car, pulling away from the curb. In the rearview mirror, Harold Westin exited the research building parking lot.

Samantha's hands tightened on the wheel, resolve hardening in her gut. One way or another, she was going to wipe that smirk off the old goat's face.

Chapter 8

The Willow Creek County Courthouse records office was a cramped, dusty box of a room, stuffed to the gills with filing cabinets and yellowing paperwork. Samantha Brewer squinted against the fluorescent glare, her eyes gritty from hours of sifting through property deeds and foreclosure notices.

Despite the exhaustion, it was worth it. Because there, buried in the fine print and legalese, she found the smoking gun she'd been searching for.

Green Acres Farm, the sprawling organic oasis that had been Ethan Green's pride and joy, had been teetering on the brink of financial ruin for months before his murder. Missed payments, defaulted loans, a staggering debt load that threatened to swallow the farm whole.

And the creditor holding the sword of Damocles over Ethan's head? None other than his own sister, Natalie Sandoval.

Samantha sat back, a grim sense of satisfaction unfurling in her gut. It all made sense now - Natalie's seething resentment, her callous dismissal of Ethan's vision. She hadn't just wanted the farm for herself. She'd needed it, with a desperation that could drive even the most upstanding citizen to unspeakable acts.

The inheritance clause was the clincher. As next of kin, Natalie stood to gain everything if Ethan defaulted on his payments. The land, the assets, the legacy of the Green family, all falling into her flawlessly manicured hands.

Ethan's death provided Natalie with motive, means, and opportunity, constituting an airtight case against her from a legal standpoint. And Samantha was determined to ensure Natalie knew she'd connected the dots, no ifs, ands or buts.

The bistro was all sleek lines and muted earth tones, a far cry from the greasy spoons and cozy diners that peppered Willow Creek's Main Street. Natalie Sandoval looked right at home amid the polished wood and artisanal flatware, her tailored suit and severe bob a perfect complement to the upscale decor.

She barely glanced up as Samantha slid into the seat across from her, her attention focused on the glowing screen of her smartphone. "You're late."

Samantha bit back a retort, reminding herself to play nice. For now. "Sorry, traffic was a bear. You know how it is."

Natalie made a noncommittal noise, finally deigning to meet Samantha's gaze. Her eyes were cool, assessing. "I have to admit, your call surprised me," Natalie said. "I assumed we'd said all there was to say about Ethan."

"Did we?" Samantha leaned forward, elbows on the table. "Because I've been doing some digging, Natalie. And it seems there's a lot you left out of our previous chat."

Natalie's expression didn't flicker, but Samantha caught the faint tightening around her eyes, the minute clench of her jaw. "I'm sure I don't know what you're talking about."

"Really?" Samantha pulled a sheaf of papers from her bag, sliding them across the table. "Then I guess these foreclosure notices are just a figment of my imagination. Funny, they've got your name all over them."

Natalie's gaze flicked to the papers, then back to Samantha. A muscle twitched in her cheek. "That was a private matter between my brother and I. It has nothing to do with his death."

"Doesn't it?" Samantha pressed. "Seems to me you had a lot to gain if Ethan went belly-up. All that prime farmland, falling right into your lap. Must've been tempting."

Natalie's nostrils flared, a crack in the impassive mask. "You have no idea what you're talking about. No idea the sacrifices I made, the things I gave up, all to keep Ethan's precious organic dream afloat."

"Oh, boo hoo." Samantha rolled her eyes. "Cry me a river, Natalie. You're not the only one who had to make hard choices. I can't help but wonder if your financial interests drove you to consider... extreme measures."

Natalie shot to her feet, her chair screeching against the tile. Heads swiveled in their direction, curious eyes taking in the unfolding drama.

"How dare you!" Natalie's voice shook with barely contained fury. "How dare you judge me, like you have any idea what it was like? Growing up always second fiddle to Ethan, the golden boy with his new-age crusades, constantly in his shadow."

She laughed, bitter and jagged. "You know, when I got into Stanford, my parents didn't even bother to read my acceptance letter. They were too busy fawning over Ethan's latest save-the-whales essay, or whatever pap he peddled that week."

Samantha frowned, a pang of unexpected sympathy welling up in her chest. She understood the feeling of being overlooked and underestimated. To feel you'd never measure up, no matter how hard you tried.

But she pushed the feeling down, steeling herself. Natalie's childhood wounds didn't justify cold-blooded murder. Nothing could.

"I'm sorry you had a rough go of it, Natalie. Really, I am." Samantha kept her voice level and reasonable. "But that doesn't change the facts. You had the most to gain from Ethan's death. And I think you know more about his fate than you're revealing."

Natalie's face contorted, an ugly mask of rage and resentment. She snatched up her water glass, hurling it to the floor in a crash of shattered crystal. Patrons gasped and muttered, edging away from the drama.

"You sanctimonious little brat," Natalie hissed, jabbing a finger at Samantha. "You think you're so smart, don't you? The hotshot reporter, come to save the day and solve the big mystery."

She leaned in close, eyes blazing. "Well, I've got news for you, Nancy Drew. You don't know a blasted thing. It's not about me or Ethan, nor about what truly happened that night."

With that, she turned on her heel and stalked out of the restaurant, leaving a trail of gawking onlookers in her wake. Samantha slumped back in her chair, heart pounding.

Well. That had gone as well as expected.

But even as the adrenaline ebbed, a kernel of doubt lodged in Samantha's gut. Natalie's reaction had been explosive, sure. But was it the fury of a guilty conscience? Or the righteous anger of the falsely accused?

Samantha didn't know. But she determined to find out, come hell or high water.

The texts started that night, a barrage of cryptic messages from a blocked number. Vague warnings, ominous hints about digging too deep, kicking hornets' nests better left undisturbed.

At first, Samantha tried to brush them off, just another crank trying to rattle her cage. But as the messages grew more insistent and more specific, a chill crept up her spine.

You're on the right track. You're searching in the wrong place.

Natalie's not the one you should be worried about. It's the people she works for.

Agrocore. Look into them. See how they deal with thorns in their side.

Agrocore. The name rang a faint bell, a half-remembered news story about industrial farming and shady business practices. Samantha fired up her laptop, fingers flying over the keys.

What she found made her blood run cold.

Agrocore was a behemoth, a multinational conglomerate with tendrils in every aspect of the global food chain. Pesticides, fertilizers, genetically modified crops - if it could be sprayed, injected, or spliced into a seed, Agrocore had a hand in it.

And they didn't appreciate competition. Especially not from small, idealistic upstarts like Ethan Green.

Samantha scrolled through article after article, a pit growing in her stomach. Tales of strong-arm tactics, of family farms driven to ruin by spurious lawsuits and cutthroat business practices. Of whistleblowers silenced, activists threatened, regulators bought and paid for.

It was a web of corruption and greed, stretching from Wall Street to the heartland. And at the center of it all, a name that made Samantha's heart stutter in her chest.

Natalie Sandoval. Senior Vice President of Operations, Agrocore Midwest Division.

The pieces fell into place with sickening clarity. Natalie's sudden interest in the Farm's finances. The foreclosure notices, timed just as Ethan's activist star was on the rise. The cold, calculated maneuvering of a corporate shark circling a wounded seal.

But had she taken the ultimate step? Had she wielded the knife herself, or merely created the conditions that made her brother's murder all but inevitable?

Samantha didn't know. But one thing was certain - Sheriff Cooper needed to hear about this, and fast.

She tucked her notes into her messenger bag and headed out to the parking lot behind her mom's house. The night was inky black, the moon a slender crescent that cast long, spindly shadows across the cracked pavement.

Samantha's boots crunched over the gravel as she made her way to Jenny's loaner Taurus. She was just digging the keys out of her pocket when the sound of an engine revving made her freeze.

A pair of blinding high beams flared in her peripheral vision. Samantha squinted against the glare as a truck roared past, its tires kicking up a spray of loose stones. She flinched, shielding her face as the gravelly pings pelted her jacket.

"What a jerk!" she shouted at the retreating taillights. Just some reckless kid with a testosterone surplus out for a joyride.

Samantha climbed into the Taurus, shaking her head in disgust. She had just pulled out onto the main road when those same high beams flared up in her rearview mirror, seriously close now.

Okay, that was weird. Samantha frowned, gripping the wheel a little tighter. She took the turn for Old Mill Road, hoping to lose her trailer in the residential streets.

No such luck. The high beams stayed glued to her rear bumper, looming like the relentless stare of a predator sighting its prey.

Samantha's pulse kicked up a notch. This was no random, reckless driver. Someone was intentionally following her, riding her tail through every turn and straightaway.

She floored the accelerator, the old sedan's engine whining in protest. The high beams grew brighter, more intense in the rearview. Samantha risked a glance over her shoulder and her heart stuttered.

The truck was so close to her she could make out the black grillwork, the meaty tires, the winking chrome accents. Close enough to read the make and model if she could just—

Wham! The front end slammed into her rear quarter panel, causing the Taurus to shake. Samantha's head whipped forward, teeth gnashing her tongue. The metallic taste of blood filled her mouth as she wrenched the wheel, struggling to maintain control.

Another bone-jarring impact, this time from the left rear. The truck was trying to run her off the road, playing a sadistic game of vehicular chicken. Samantha screamed, knuckles whitening on the wheel as she fought against the crushing momentum.

She glimpsed the driver's silhouette, all hard angles and cold intent. Whoever was behind that wheel wasn't messing around.

With a savage wrench, the truck rammed into her again. The Taurus careened sideways, tires clawing for purchase on the gravel shoulder. Samantha wrestled with the steering wheel, unable to regain control as the sedan plowed off the road into the shallow ditch on the left.

The Taurus' tires flung up clods of dirt and grass before finally rolling to a stop, tilted but undamaged. Samantha's heart thundered in her ears, adrenaline spiking as she realized how close she'd just come to a serious crash.

In her side mirror, she saw the truck's brake lights get smaller as it tore away from the scene toward Mason City, engines snarling in the night.

Samantha collapsed back against her seat, chest heaving. Her whole body trembled with delayed shock and relief at being alive. That driver obviously wanted her dead - or at the very least, scared into abandoning her investigation completely.

Well, they had another thing coming if they thought some amateur scare tactics would deter her. Samantha's jaw set in a defiant line as she gingerly pulled the Taurus back onto the road and pointed it toward town.

She glanced at the clock on the dashboard - nearly 2am. Cooper would be fast asleep like any sane person at this hour. Despite her eagerness to fill him in right away, it could wait until morning. No sense in rousting him from bed tonight.

Samantha let out a shaky breath and steered the Taurus toward her mother's house. She needed to get somewhere secure, get her wits about her after that terrifying ordeal.

At Delores' place, Samantha secured the door with a heavy dresser shoved in front of it. Paranoid maybe, but after tonight's events, she didn't feel like taking any chances.

Climbing into bed, she stared at the ceiling, replaying the chase over and over in her mind's eye. The truck's malicious high beams, the jolting impacts as it tried to force her off the road. She shuddered, fresh adrenaline prickling over her skin.

This was no prank, no idle threat. Someone had just tried to kill her. Because she was getting too close to the truth about Ethan's murder.

Well, forget that. She'd be stupid if she'd let a homicidal redneck in a pickup stop her from finding justice. First thing tomorrow, she was marching right into Cooper's office and laying it all out—the case against Natalie, the threats, the blocked number and tonight's terrifying chase.

Regardless of the mule's preferences, he had to take her seriously now. This killer meant business, and Samantha had no intention of being their next victim.

The sheriff's station was a buzz of activity when Samantha pushed through the doors the next morning, her body still aching from the previous night's harrowing chase. Uniformed deputies milled about with purposeful strides. She ignored the curious glances and muttered asides as she made her way to Cooper's office.

He glanced up as she barged in without knocking, a scowl already forming on his craggy face. "Good heavens, Brewer. Don't you ever—"

"Can it, Sheriff." Samantha cut him off, planting her palms on his desk. "Some psycho in a truck almost killed me last night by running me off the blasted road," Samantha explained. "And I'm willing to bet it has everything to do with me sniffing around Ethan's murder."

Cooper's bushy eyebrows shot up, but she didn't give him a chance to respond, launching into the whole sordid tale - the threats via text, the chilling blocked number call, and finally the harrowing chase that had ended with her vehicle spinning into a ditch.

"So you see?" she finished, breathless. "I'm onto something big here, and someone is dead set on stopping me before I can crack it wide open. I've got a lead, Sheriff. A big one that could blow this entire case apart."

Cooper leaned back in his chair, arms crossed over his barrel chest as he appraised her with those beady cop's eyes. "Is that so? And what earth-shattering revelation have you stumbled on this time?"

Samantha took a deep breath, organizing her thoughts. "It's Natalie Sandoval. Ethan's sister. I think she's involved, maybe even the mastermind behind the whole thing."

She laid out the evidence - the foreclosure notices, the corporate connections, the cutthroat tactics. Cooper listened with a stony expression, not a flicker of reaction on his grizzled face.

When she finished, breathless and eager, he merely stared at her for a long moment. Then, to her utter shock, he barked out in laughter.

"Good grief, Brewer. You really are something else, you know that?" He shook his head, a patronizing smile playing over his lips. "A couple of legal documents, some shady business dealings, and suddenly it's a vast corporate conspiracy?"

Samantha gaped at him, disbelief warring with outrage. "Are you kidding me right now? Did you not hear a single word I said? Someone nearly killed me last night, Sheriff! I'm getting too close to the truth about who had Ethan murdered!"

Cooper held up a hand, cutting her off. "What I heard is a lot of baseless speculation and circumstantial bunk. You've got no actual proof, no smoking gun. Just a lot of dramatic theories cobbled together from thin air."

He leaned forward, eyes hardening. "Maybe some reckless yahoo tried to run you off the road. I'll take an incident report, make sure it's on file. But that don't make it connected to your little murder investigation."

Samantha's hands clenched into fists, nails biting into her palms. The urge to scream, to rage against Cooper's willful blindness, was almost overwhelming.

But she forced it down, gritting her teeth until her jaw ached. Losing her cool wouldn't help Ethan. And it wouldn't persuade Cooper to fulfill his job.

"Fine," she bit out, the word tasting like acid on her tongue. "Take the report. But don't think for one second I'm giving up on this, with or without your help. I'll find the truth about what happened to Ethan. Even if you keep burying your head in the sand."

Cooper snorted, already turning back to his paperwork. "You do what you must, Brewer. Just stay out of my way and avoid trouble while doing so. Now go see Sergeant Kester at the desk and he will take your report."

Samantha turned on her heel, striding out of his office with her head held high. She found the Desk Sergeant and 90 minutes later; she left the station and wouldn't give Cooper the satisfaction of seeing her break. Not again.

But as the door swung shut behind her, the tears she'd been holding back fell, hot and bitter, on her cheeks.

She was on the cusp, incredibly close to finding the justice Ethan deserved, the closure his memory demanded. And with each dead end, each ignorant roadblock like Cooper, that sense of failure weighed heavier on her soul.

But she couldn't, wouldn't, give up. Not when the truth was almost within her grasp. Not when Natalie Sandoval's shadowy corporate masters still had secrets to burn.

One way or another, Samantha was determined to expose them all. Or die trying.

Chapter 9

The next few days passed in a blur of manic activity. Samantha retrieved her Honda from Bucky's Auto Repair, relieved when the gruff mechanic mentioned her insurance had covered the cost of replacing the slashed tires with a casual grunt.

"Durn kids these days, no respect for other folks' property," he groused, handing over her keys.

Samantha managed a tight smile, not bothering to disabuse him of the assumption it had been a random act of vandalism. Let's not focus on the negative implications.

She spent her nights studying the case files, the corporate records, anything that could reveal more about Natalie's murky dealings. A relentless cycle of following up on leads occupied her days, tracking down witnesses, and piecing together the ever-expanding web of suspicion surrounding Ethan's death.

Nights and days blurred for Samantha, making them indistinguishable. She existed in a permanent state of exhaustion and single-minded focus, all other concerns falling away until only the truth mattered.

It was a chance text from Jenny that finally broke the cycle, a rushed message about some kind of breakthrough from an unlikely source. Samantha had dropped everything to meet her friend at the sheriff's station, the manic glaze in her eyes finally clearing as the promise of progress reinvigorated her weary bones.

Which was how she squinted at a grainy monitor, Cooper's bulk looming beside her as the muted security footage played out.

The video was timestamped only a few hours after Ethan's estimated death, the silent camera trained on the deserted country lane that led to Green Acres Farm. The grainy footage flickered on the ancient TV screen, a black-and-white tableau of empty fields and deserted gravel roads.

Samantha Brewer leaned forward, eyes straining for any hint of movement, any clue that might break Ethan Green's murder wide open.

There. A flash of motion at the edge of the frame, a vehicle kicking up dust as it tore down the country lane. Samantha jabbed the pause button, heart hammering against her ribs.

"Sheriff Cooper." Her voice was tight, controlled. "Can you zoom in on that truck? I need to see the plates."

Cooper grunted, fiddling with the remote. The image stuttered, then exploded into pixelated chaos as he jabbed at the buttons. "Doggone newfangled technology. Give me a good old-fashioned stakeout any day."

After an eternity of blurred shapes and staticky snow, the picture finally resolved. Samantha squinted at the fuzzy license plate, a thrill of recognition zipping down her spine.

She knew that truck. Had seen it parked outside the ramshackle apartment on Elm Street, rusting hubcaps and faded green paint job as familiar as her own face in the mirror.

The ride belonged to Lucas Fernandez. And according to the timestamp, he'd been hightailing it away from Ethan's farm at 4:30 AM. A full hour before the coroner's estimated time of death.

Samantha sat back, mind whirring. Lucas insisted he was home all night, that he hadn't set foot on Green Acres until well after sunrise.

What compelled him to speed down that road like the devil himself was in hot pursuit? More importantly, what was he running from?

The drive to Lucas' place was a blur, Samantha's knuckles white on the steering wheel. She scarcely noticed the shabby houses and overgrown yards flashing by, her thoughts consumed by the implications of that incriminating video footage.

Lucas had lied to her. Straight to her face, with those soulful brown eyes wide and earnest. The realization stung more than anticipated, a barb of betrayal under her skin.

She thought of the easy camaraderie they'd shared, the sense of kinship forged over long days in the fields and late nights poring over Ethan's idealistic plans. Had it all been an act? A carefully crafted persona to throw her off the scent?

The anger carried her up the rickety stairs to Lucas' door, propelling her fist against the weathered wood with a force that shook the frame. She knew she should handle this with more finesse, more subtlety. But the fury was a living thing inside her, wild and raw and demanding release.

The door cracked open, a sliver of shadow and wariness. Lucas' face appeared, confusion melting into dread as he registered Samantha's thunderous expression.

"Sam? What are you doing here?"

"Don't play dumb with me, Lucas." She shouldered past him, ignoring his spluttered protest. The apartment was dim and cramped, the air thick with the sour tang of old sweat and stale cigarettes.

Samantha rounded on him, jabbing a finger at his chest. "I saw the footage. Your truck, leaving Ethan's farm at 4:30 in the morning, right around the time of his death."

Lucas blanched, his eyes darting away from hers. "That's... that's not possible. I was here, asleep. I didn't leave until after sunrise to start the morning chores."

"Don't lie to me." Samantha's voice cracked like a whip, making him flinch. "I talked to your neighbor, Mrs. Kowalski. She witnessed you peel out of here like a bat out of hell around 4 AM. So I'm going to ask you again. Where were you that night?"

Lucas sagged onto the threadbare couch, head in his hands. For a long moment, he said nothing; the silence broken only by the hum of the ancient refrigerator in the kitchen.

Then, he spoke with a deliberate slowness. His voice was low and raw, scraped thin with anguish.

"I couldn't sleep. Ethan's words kept echoing in my head, the disgust in his voice when he figured out what I'd done."

He looked up at Samantha, eyes haunted. "He called me a traitor. A slave to the poison peddlers. Said I'd betrayed everything he'd taught me, everything we'd worked for."

Samantha's gut clenched. The illegal pesticides. The bitter fight that had left Lucas shattered and Ethan unflinching in his righteous fury.

"I had to talk to him," Lucas whispered. "To make him understand. I wasn't... I wasn't trying to hurt anyone. My sole aim was to save the crop in order to sustain the farm. For him. For his dream."

He dragged a shaking hand over his face. "So I drove over there, before dawn. I intended to apologize, to beg for another chance. But when I got there..."

His voice cracked, a shattered sound. "He was already dead. Lying there in the cabbage patch, blood everywhere. I searched for a pulse, attempted CPR, anything. But it was too late."

Samantha's head spun, the room tilting precariously around her. Lucas' story made sense. The timing, the motive for the predawn visit. Despite everything, an unsettling sense of wrongness persisted within her.

"Why didn't you call the police?" She demanded. "If you found him like that, why not report it immediately?"

Lucas flinched as if she'd struck him. The shame of his troubled youth weighed on him. "I panicked. I thought they'd only see the delinquent, never believe I was innocent."

Samantha stepped back, mind racing. Lucas' juvenile record was news to her, a crucial piece of the puzzle that cast everything in a darker light. Hadn't Ethan mentioned reforming a troubled youth? Giving a second chance to a kid from a rough background?

She thought of the murder weapon, the sleek Japanese knife that had ended Ethan's life. On a hunch, she moved to the kitchenette, yanking open drawers with rising urgency.

There, nestled among the mismatched utensils and takeout chopsticks, was an invoice. For a Shun Classic 8-inch vegetable knife. Ordered two weeks before Ethan's death.

Samantha's hands trembled ever so slightly, bagging the paper in a ziplock, fighting the urge to confront Lucas immediately. She needed to do this by the book, to build an airtight case before she showed her hand.

"I have to go," she forced, too wary to speak further. "I know I can't make you stay. But please, don't leave town until I can figure this out."

She could feel his stricken gaze boring into her back as she fled the apartment, the suffocating walls and stale air. But she couldn't meet his gaze, couldn't face the broken plea in those soft brown eyes.

Not yet. Not until she knew the truth.

The next few hours passed in a haze of manic activity; Samantha's mind was laser-focused on the task at hand. She pored over maps of the farm, calculating distances and timelines with a fevered intensity.

She scoured online databases, piecing together the shards of Lucas' troubled past into a mosaic of violence and instability. The assault charges, the knife fight that had nearly claimed another boy's life. The repeated stints in juvie, the sealed records and faded mugshots.

It all fit. The timeline, the motive, the means. Lucas had the skills to overpower Ethan, the intimate knowledge of his routines and vulnerabilities. And he had the darkness in him, the capacity for brutal violence that he'd tried so hard to bury.

Even so, a part of Samantha resisted. The part that shared laughter with Lucas in the hayloft, that had seen the gentle way he tended the seedlings and soothed the anxious livestock. The part that couldn't reconcile the lost boy with the cold-blooded killer.

She pushed the doubts away, steeling herself for what came next. Justice for Ethan. That was all that mattered now.

Sheriff Cooper was unusually grim as Samantha laid out the evidence, his weathered face set in lines of weary resignation. He'd known Lucas since he was a scrappy kid running wild in the streets, all bravado and bruised knuckles. It's difficult to see that boy as a murderer, betraying the man who'd provided him with everything.

But the facts were undeniable. The knife, the interrupted timeline. The history of violence, etched into Lucas's very bones.

"Alright," Cooper said at last, heaving himself to his feet with a groan. "I'll bring him in. Have a chat, see what else he's hiding."

Samantha nodded, relief and dread churning in her gut. She'd known this was coming, had orchestrated it with all the ruthless efficiency of a prosecutor. Despite that, a part of her quailed at the idea of Lucas in handcuffs, in a dank cell with his demons.

What if she was mistaken? What if there was a crucial element she had missed in her hasty rush to judgment?

But doubts were no longer relevant at this point. With Lucas's arrest inevitable, Samantha could only watch the wheels of justice turn.

The interrogation room was cold, the chill of bureaucratic indifference seeping from the cinderblock walls. Samantha watched from behind the one-way glass, her presence in the restricted observation room a rare concession from Sheriff Cooper.

After pushing back against her civilian investigation at every turn, he had ultimately granted her access in begrudging recognition of the key evidence she had unearthed against Lucas Fernandez. She watched as Lucas crumbled, his denials and justifications giving way to choked sobs of despair.

"I bought the knife," he admitted, voice small and broken. "I was going to give it to Ethan as a peace offering. To show commitment to doing things his way, no matter what."

He looked up at Cooper with pleading eyes, tears tracking through the grime on his cheeks. "But I promise you, I never used it. I never hurt him. When I got there that morning, he was already gone."

Cooper leaned forward, a shark scenting blood. "Then where were you at 5 AM, Lucas? Because your timeline doesn't add up. What aren't you telling us?"

Lucas shook his head aggressively, retreating into himself like a wounded animal. "I want a lawyer," he whispered. "I'm not saying anything else without a lawyer."

Samantha's heart sank, frustration warring with a strange sense of relief. A lawyer would slow things down, giving her time to untangle the knots in her gut. Time to be sure.

She was reaching for her phone, fingers itching to call Jake and vent, when it buzzed with an incoming message. Unknown number, no caller ID.

Her blood ran cold as she read the text, a chill skating down her spine.

"You're on the right track. But the farmhand isn't the only one involved. Someone else pulled the strings that night. And they're still at large."

Samantha stared at the words until they blurred, a sick dread settling in her bones. If Lucas wasn't the sole culprit, if there lurked another figure in the shadows, a puppet master pulling his strings...

Then this was far from over. And Ethan's killer was still out there, waiting for their moment to strike.

Samantha gripped the phone until her knuckles ached, resolve hardening into a cold, sharp fury.

Chapter 10

The soon ending County Fair raged on and was a riot of color and noise, a swirling kaleidoscope of flashing lights and shrieking laughter. Samantha Brewer wove through the crowd, dodging sticky-fingered children and overstuffed teddy bears.

She was on a mission, and it had nothing to do with funnel cakes or rigged carnival games. She was here to observe, to gather intel on her prime suspects; to observe who smiled too wide and laughed a little too loud.

But one face remained her utmost priority to avoid. A voice, after all these years, that weakened her knees and raced her heart.

"Samantha! Hey, Samantha!"

Great! Too late.

Jake Emerson jogged toward her, all tousled hair and boyish grin. He was wearing a faded flannel and scuffed work boots, looking every inch the rugged farm boy she'd fallen for back in high school.

Samantha's heart stuttered in her chest, a traitorous flutter of nostalgia and longing. She steeled herself, pasting on a bright smile as he reached her.

"Jake, hey. Enjoying the fair?"

He shrugged, hands shoved in his pockets. "It's alright. Same old, same old. But I was hoping to run into you, actually. Can we talk?"

Samantha's stomach swooped, a sickening lurch of apprehension. Nothing good ever came from those four brief words.

"I don't know, Jake. I'm kind of in the middle of something..."

"Please, Sam," he begged with an earnest gaze in his eyes. "Just for a minute. There's something I must share with you."

Against her better judgment, Samantha nodded. "Okay. Lead the way."

Jake grinned, relieved, and took her hand. Samantha tried to ignore the electric thrill that raced up her arm at the contact, the way her fingers fit perfectly with his.

He led her away from the crowds, toward the muted hush of the livestock barn. The smell of hay and manure was thick in the air, mingling with the faint ozone tang of impending rain.

Jake stopped in an empty stall, turning to face her. His expression was surprisingly serious, a furrow between his brows.

"Sam, I... I've longed to express this. Considering everything that has occurred, including Ethan, the murder, and your return to town... I didn't know how."

Samantha's heart was in her throat, her palms slick with sweat. "Jake, what are you talking about?"

He took a deep breath, squaring his shoulders. "I'm still in love with you, Samantha. I never stopped. And I know it's crazy, and the timing couldn't be worse, but... I can't keep pretending I don't feel this way. Not anymore."

Samantha's mouth fell open, a choked sound of disbelief eluding her lips. Of all the things she'd expected him to say, this wasn't even close.

"Jake, I... I don't know what to say. You're engaged. To Heather. And I'm in the middle of a murder investigation, for heaven's sake. This is... it's impossible."

Jake shook his head, stepping closer. His hands came up to frame her face, gentle but insistent. "It's not impossible, Sam. It's the only thing that makes sense. Heather and I... it was never real. A post high school crush that spiraled. I already intended to end things with her before you showed up."

Samantha's head was spinning, her heart a wild drumbeat in her ears. This couldn't be happening. It was too much, too fast.

She stepped back, breaking his hold on her. "Jake, I can't do this right now. I need time to think, to process. Everything is so messed up, with Ethan and Lucas and the farm... I can't add a love triangle to the mix."

Jake's face fell, but he nodded. "I understand. I shouldn't have sprung this on you, not with everything else going on. But I needed you to know, Sam. I needed you to know that I'm here, that I never stopped loving you. And when you're ready... I'll be waiting."

Turning away, he left Samantha alone in the barn's shadows. She pressed a shaking hand to her chest, feeling the wild thunder of her heart beneath her palm.

What was she supposed to do now?

"HE SAID WHAT?!"

Delores Brewer almost spilled her tea, eyes wide with scandalized delight. Samantha groaned, slumping back in her chair on the front porch.

"He said he's still in love with me. That he broke up with Heather, that he wants to start over. Can you believe it?"

Delores pursed her lips, setting down her china cup with a delicate clink. "Well, I can't say I'm entirely surprised, dear. That boy has been carrying a torch for you since you were knee high to a grasshopper."

Samantha blinked, nonplussed. "What? How do you know that?"

Her mother waved a dismissive hand. "Oh, please. A blind man could see it. The way he looks at you, finding excuses to be around whenever you're in town. It's as plain as the nose on your face."

Samantha's mind whirled, revisiting every interaction she'd had with Jake since coming back to Willow Creek. The lingering glances, the too-casual touches. He was consistently present and reliable whenever she needed him.

Was she truly that oblivious? Was she deliberately blind or too afraid to see what was directly before her?

Delores leaned forward, patting Samantha's knee with a sympathetic hand. "Honey, I know you've got a lot on your plate right now. I'm not suggesting you should go run off to Vegas and elope with the boy. But... don't be hasty to shut the door on love, either. Life's too short for regrets."

Samantha swallowed hard, a lump rising in her throat. She thought back to the last time she'd seen Jake before leaving for college, their bittersweet goodbye under the starry night sky at Lover's Lookout.

"I'll wait for you," he'd whispered, his breath hot against her ear. "As long as it takes, Sam. You're my forever girl."

She'd laughed it off then, too young and restless to believe in forevers. However, with the weight of years and sorrows between them... perhaps he'd been onto something after all.

"Thanks, Mom." Samantha managed a watery smile. "I'll think about it, I promise. But right now... I need to focus on finding Ethan's killer. Everything else will have to wait."

Delores nodded, a knowing glint in her eye. "Of course, dear. You do what you need to do. But remember... the heart wants what it wants. And sometimes, that's the only truth that matters."

LATER THAT NIGHT, THE stars were a glittering canopy above Lover's Lookout, the inky sky stretching out forever in every direction. Samantha sat on the hood of Jake's battered pickup truck, knees hugged to her chest. Am I doing the right thing? Mom said to follow my heart.

He sat beside her on the truck's hood, a respectful distance between them, yet still close enough for Samantha to be very aware of his presence.

"I'm glad you called," he whispered, breaking the comfortable silence. "I wasn't sure you would, after... everything."

Samantha shrugged, picking at a loose thread on her jeans. "I wasn't sure either. But I couldn't stop thinking about what you said at the fair. About us."

Jake turned to face her, his eyes glinting in the starlight. "And? What did you decide?"

Samantha took a deep breath, her heart a wild thing in her chest. "I decided... that I'm tired of running. From this town, from my past. From you."

She reached out, lacing her fingers with his. "I'm not saying it'll be easy, Jake. I'm a mess and this case is a nightmare. We have a lot of baggage to sort through. But... I want to try. I want to see if there's still something between us."

Jake's grin was brighter than the moon, his entire face alight with joy. "That's all I needed to hear, darlin'. We'll take it slow, figure it out as we go. But I'm in this, Sam. I'm all in."

In a rush of nostalgia, Jake leaned in and gave Samantha a gentle kiss on the cheek. A few hoots and cheers erupted from nearby cars at Lover's Lookout, teenagers playfully whistling at the old high school sweethearts sharing an innocent moment. Samantha felt her cheeks flush from Jake's affectionate gesture, but mostly from the playful hollers of the onlookers treating them like love-struck kids again.

For a moment, she let herself forget. Forget the murder, the secrets, the tangled web of lies and betrayal that had brought her back to Willow Creek. In that moment, Jake stood alone, surrounded by stars, and the promise of a future she had never imagined possible.

But reality shattered her tranquility with the shrill ring of her cell phone. Samantha reluctantly pulled away, fumbling for the device with clumsy fingers.

"Brewer," she answered, forcing herself to focus despite Jake's distracting presence beside her.

"It's Cooper." The Sheriff's voice was strained. "We got the lab results back on that fertilizer sample from Ethan's crops. You're gonna want to see this."

Samantha's blood ran cold, the dreamy haze of the moment shattering like glass. She glanced at Jake, at the soft smile playing around his lips, and felt her heart sink to her toes.

"The results showed traces of a proprietary fertilizer blend that seem to link back to the Emerson farm operation. It's pretty damning stuff, Samantha. You'll want to see it for yourself."

Samantha's mind raced, the Emersons' struggling farm and ongoing feuds with Ethan's organic business churning in her thoughts. Could this evidence somehow tie back to Jake's operation?

"Wait, are you saying this evidence could implicate the Emerson farm? Jake's operation?"

"Yes. And we'll be exploring this further."

"Thanks for that update, Sheriff. I'll swing by if I need more details."

"You do that. Don't delay for too long. Time's wasting."

"Fine," she said through gritted teeth, breaking off the call by pressing her finger on the screen. She slid off the hood of the truck, not meeting Jake's eyes.

"Sam? What's going on?" He sounded confused, a little hurt. Samantha steeled herself, forcing the words out past the sudden tightness in her throat.

"That was Sheriff Cooper. He's got a new lead on Ethan's murder. And Jake... it points right to you."

THE SUN PEEPED OVER the horizon, the sky a pale wash of gray and pink, when Samantha confronted Jake at his family's farm. She found him in the barn, mucking out stalls with a grim determination.

"Why didn't you tell me?" Her voice was rougher than she intended, scraped raw with betrayal. "About the fertilizer, about your farm's financial troubles. About your motive to remove Ethan."

Jake stiffened, his shoulders going rigid beneath his sweat-stained t-shirt. He gradually turned to face her, his expression unreadable.

"I don't know what you're talking about, Sam."

Samantha scoffed, crossing her arms over her chest. "Don't play dumb, Jake. It doesn't suit you well. The Sheriff found traces of a custom pesticide on Ethan's crops, one that's only used by your family's farm. I conducted some investigation myself. Seems like the Emersons have been struggling for years, ever since Ethan started his organic crusade. You were hemorrhaging money, losing contracts left and right. Motive, means, and opportunity, all wrapped up in a tidy little package."

Jake's jaw clenched, a muscle ticking in his cheek. "You don't know what you're talking about, Sam. Yes, we've had some hard times. Yes, Ethan's preaching didn't exactly help matters. But I would never, never hurt him. He was my friend, for heaven's sake!"

"Was he?" Samantha stepped closer, her voice dropping to a hiss. "Or was he just an obstacle, a roadblock on your path to prosperity? Tell me, Jake. Explain why I shouldn't march right to the sheriff's office and tell Cooper to arrest you right now."

For a long moment, Jake said nothing. He just stared at her, his eyes dark and fathomless in the weak morning light. He extended his hand and tenderly cupped her face in his broad, callused hand.

"Because you know me, Sam. Better than anyone. Deep inside, you know I could never do something like this. Regardless how bad the situation got or how desperate I was... I'm not a killer. I'm not that man."

Samantha swallowed hard, her throat tight and aching. She wanted to believe him. She desperately desired it with every fiber of her being. But the facts... the facts were damning. And she couldn't let her feelings, her history with this man, cloud her judgment. Not when justice for Ethan hung in the balance.

She stepped back, breaking his touch. "Then explain it to me, Jake. Explain the fertilizer, the money problems. Give me something, anything, to prove your innocence since at the moment... all signs point to guilty."

Jake's face hardened, a shutter slamming down behind his eyes. "I don't have to explain myself to you, Samantha. I don't owe you anything. If you won't trust me past your own suspicions and preconceptions... perhaps we've nothing left to say to each other after all."

With that, he turned on his heel and stalked out of the barn, leaving Samantha alone with the sour stench of manure and the bitter taste of regret on her tongue.

She was in a daze as she mechanically investigated till evening. She interviewed witnesses, reviewed case files, followed up on leads that went nowhere.

Her mind remained in the barn, where Jake's betrayal and hurtful gaze lingered. When he walked away, perhaps forever.

As the sun set, painting the sky in shades of fire and gold, Samantha found herself parked outside the Emerson farm once more. She told herself she was just tying up loose ends, following protocol. But she couldn't shake the feeling that she was missing something. That there was more to the story than it seemed.

She nearly gave up, to turn the key in the ignition and drive away, when she saw it. A flicker of movement in the upstairs farmhouse window, a shadow darting behind the curtain.

Her heart in her throat, Samantha crept closer, keeping to the lengthening shadows. As she watched, Jake emerged from the house, a stack of papers clutched in his hand.

He appeared furtive, glancing around as if to make sure he was alone. Then, with a grim set to his jaw, he strode to the burn barrel behind the barn and began feeding the papers into the flames, one by one.

Samantha's blood ran cold. Those papers... they could be evidence. Proof of Jake's guilt, of his involvement in Ethan's murder. And he was destroying them right before her eyes.

It's possible she made a sound, a gasp or a cry. In an instant, Jake's head snapped up, his eyes locking onto hers across the darkening yard.

They briefly locked eyes, the only sound being the crackling flames. Then, Jake's face twisted into a mask of fury, and he stalked toward her, purpose in every line of his body.

Samantha turned to run, her heart hammering in her chest. But it was too late. Jake's hand closed around her arm, yanking her back to face him.

"What are you doing here, Samantha?" His voice was a low growl, his fingers biting into her skin. "Spying on me? Trying to catch me in the act of some imagined crime?"

Samantha struggled in his grip, fear and anger warring in her gut. "I'm trying to find the truth, Jake. The truth about what happened to Ethan, about your part in it all. What about those papers? Those papers could be the key. Why else would you destroy them, unless you had something to hide?"

Jake barked a harsh laugh, shaking his head. "You just can't let it go, can you? Can't accept that perhaps, just maybe, I'm not the monster you've built me up to be in your head. Well, I've got news for you, Samantha. Those papers? They were old receipts, tax documents. No connection with Ethan or the farm. I was just clearing out some junk, like I do every month."

Samantha stared at him, doubt creeping in like a cancer. Could he be telling the truth? Could she have allowed her suspicions and her need for answers to overshadow her judgment completely?

"I don't... I don't know what to believe anymore, Jake." Her voice cracked, tears stinging the backs of her eyes. "I want to trust you, I do. But there's so much evidence and numerous coincidences..."

"Coincidences aren't proof, Sam." Jake's voice softened, his grip on her arm loosening. "Your evidence is only circumstantial, at best. You want to know the truth? I loved Ethan like a brother. I would've done anything for him, absolutely anything. And that you would think of me as capable of... of that..."

He broke off, his voice choked with emotion. Samantha's heart clenched, a wave of shame and doubt crashing over her. Had she been so blinded by her need for answers, so desperate to find meaning in Ethan's senseless death, that she'd let herself believe the worst of the man she once loved?

"Jake, I..." She reached for him, her fingers brushing his sleeve. "I'm sorry. My intention was never to make you feel accused or untrusted by me. I just... Knowing the truth is essential for me. I need to understand what happened to Ethan, why someone wanted to hurt him. And I thought... I thought maybe you could help me. That we could figure it out together."

Jake yanked his arm away, his face twisting into a mask of hurt and anger. "Help you? Is that what you call this, Samantha? Snooping around my property, digging through my past, looking for any scrap of evidence to hang me with? You're not looking for the truth. You're searching for a scapegoat, someone to blame this on so you can walk away with a clear conscience."

Samantha flinched as if he'd slapped her, tears blurring her vision. "That's not true, Jake. I promise, I never meant to hurt you. I just... Ethan deserves better and I need to step up. No matter the price, I must find justice for him."

"Justice?" Jake laughed a harsh, bitter sound. "There is no justice, Sam. Not in this world, not in this town. Ethan's dead, and no amount of digging or accusing or self-righteous crusading is going to bring him back. All you're doing is tearing open old wounds, making enemies of the people who care about you most."

He turned away from her, his shoulders rigid with tension. "I think you should go, Samantha. Go back to your big city, your fancy podcast. Go find someone else's life to ruin. Because I'm done being your punching bag, your suspect of the week. I'm done with all of it."

Samantha opened her mouth. A thousand apologies, a thousand pleas crowded her throat. But Jake was already walking away, his boots crunching on the gravel into the lengthening shadows.

The air felt heavy with the weight of unspoken words and shattered trust. Samantha watched Jake disappear into the shadows, his broad shoulders tense with anger and hurt. But it was too late now. Too late for apologies, for second chances. Jake was gone, and she was alone. Alone with her guilt, her regrets.

She forced herself to turn away, each step back towards her car feeling leaden and hollow. The engine rumbled in protest, as if echoing the tumult that had raged inside her. Samantha pulled away from the Emerson farm, tires crunching on the gravel drive.

The ride home passed in a blur of streetlights and recriminations. Her mind replayed the confrontation on a loop, Jake's words piercing her heart like arrows. Was she too quick to accuse, too eager to cast him as the villain in this sordid tale? The kernel of doubt took root, threatening to unravel her unwavering determination.

As she pulled up to the old two-story home, Samantha felt hopelessly adrift. She climbed the porch steps like someone walking to the gallows and entered the door into the hushed interior.

The house was quiet save for the soft ticking of the wall clock in the gloom. Shadows stretched across Samantha's room, where she hunched over her notes. The dim light of her desk lamp illuminated the pile of papers. Delores had retired for the evening, and the silence was almost total—a stark contrast to the chaos Samantha's thoughts had caused.

She turned over her conversation with Jake, each word, each accusation heavy with weight. She second-guessed, her mind spiraling through the labyrinth of case details. Her fingers mindlessly tapped at the desk, the rhythm disjointed, discordant with the anxiety that had risen.

The clock chimed ten—ten somber notes that echoed through the house, seeming to signal the finality of the day's events. Samantha sighed and leaned back, rubbing her bloodshot eyes. The tension of the day clung to her muscles, taut and unyielding. She was about to stand and stretch when it happened.

The sudden shatter of breaking glass ripped through the quiet, the noise an explosion in the stillness. Samantha jerked up, her chair clattering to the floor behind her. Her heart lurched as she stared at the window—the blinds swaying slightly with a breeze that carried the scent of fresh-turned earth and the faint sound of crickets.

A rock, innocuous but for the implicit threat it bore, lay on the floor amidst the glittering fragments of her window. Wrapped around it, a scrap of paper featured a hastily scrawled message: "Stop digging or the next one won't miss."

Delores's voice, roused by the commotion, called out from her bedroom, tinged with alarm. "Samantha? Samantha, what's happened?"

She didn't answer right away. She froze, her eyes fixed on the rock. The message could only come from someone privy to her investigation—undoubtably a warning. But who sent it? Was Jake that upset to do something like this, fresh off their heated confrontation?

Swallowing her fear, she finally called back, "It's nothing, Mom. Just a broken window. Probably some kids pulling a prank. Go back to sleep; I'll handle it."

Delores didn't protest, and within moments, the silence resettled. But for Samantha, any sense of peace was irrevocably shattered. Her heart still hammered in her chest as she surveyed the glittering shards of glass on the floor.

Samantha embraced her trembling form, her quivering limbs clutching her torso as she fixated upon the shattered shards and jagged gouges marring the floor.

Samantha rose on unsteady legs, bracing herself against the desk as she caught her breath. Her gaze darted around the room, taking in the shattered window, the menacing rock, the scrap of paper with its chilling threat.

She felt exposed, vulnerable. I think recording this incident is necessary. The Sheriff needs to know about this. With that, she picked her phone up and dialed 911.

SAMANTHA STOOD ON THE porch, her arms enveloping herself as she watched the deputies return to their squad cars parked at the curb. The blue lights atop the vehicles flashed sporadically, casting an eerie glow across the quiet residential street. The occasional crackle of radio traffic emanated from the cars, a stark reminder of the seriousness of the situation.

Deputy Mitchell, a tall, broad-shouldered man with a neatly trimmed mustache, paused at the bottom of the steps. He turned to face Samantha, his expression a mix of concern and reassurance. "Miss Brewer, we've taken the rock and the note into evidence. Our forensics team will examine them for any fingerprints or other clues that might help us identify the perpetrator."

Samantha nodded, her gaze flickering to the shattered window. The jagged edges of the glass glinted in the moonlight, a haunting reminder of the violation she had experienced. "Thank you, Deputy Mitchell. I appreciate you and your partner coming out so quickly."

The deputy's partner, a younger woman with short, cropped hair, joined him at the bottom of the steps. "We'll be patrolling the area throughout the rest of the night, Miss Brewer. If you see or hear anything suspicious, call us immediately."

Samantha managed a small, grateful smile. "I will. Thank you both again."

Deputy Mitchell tipped his hat, a gesture of respect and reassurance. "Try to get some rest, Miss Brewer. We'll be in touch if we have any updates on the investigation."

With that, the deputies climbed into their respective squad cars; the doors closing with a solid thunk. The engines rumbled to life, and the vehicles pulled away from the curb, their blue lights fading into the distance as they disappeared down the street.

Samantha remained on the porch for a moment longer, her gaze fixed on the spot where the police parked their cars. The night air felt cool against her skin, a stark contrast to the adrenaline that still coursed through her veins. She drew in a deep, steadying breath, trying to calm her racing thoughts.

The vandalism and intimidation had rattled her, shaking her confidence in the safety of her own home. But Samantha knew she couldn't let fear dictate her actions. She had a responsibility to Ethan, to uncover the truth behind his murder and bring his killer to justice.

With a final glance at the shattered window, Samantha turned and headed back inside, closing the door firmly behind her. Inside the house, the soft ticking of the living room wall clock broke the silence. She made her way up the stairs, her footsteps muffled by the thick carpet.

In her bedroom, Samantha sank down onto the edge of the bed, her shoulders sagging with exhaustion. The events of the night replayed in her mind, a dizzying whirlwind of shattered glass and menacing threats. She knew she should try to get some rest, but her mind remained restless.

Instead, she reached for her notebook, flipping it open to a blank page. With a deep breath, Samantha wrote, documenting every detail of the incident, from the sound of the breaking glass to the words scrawled on the note. She realized that every piece of information, no matter how small, could be crucial in unraveling the mystery of Ethan's death.

As she wrote, Samantha felt a sense of purpose settle over her, a steely determination that cut through the fear and uncertainty. She stood tall, defiant against any attempts to break her. She would continue to dig, to push, to fight for the truth, no matter the cost.

With a last flourish of her pen, Samantha closed the notebook, a sense of resolve settling in her chest. She knew the road ahead would be difficult, fraught with danger and deception. But she was ready to face whatever challenges lay ahead, armed knowing that she was fighting for something bigger than herself.

Violated in the supposed safety of her mother's home, Samantha collapsed onto the rumpled sheets. She pulled the covers up around her like armor, shielding her from the encroaching shadows.

But no matter how tightly she wrapped herself in the bedding's thin barrier, she could not escape the creeping tendrils of fear. She lay awake, sheets tangling around her restless limbs as her mind raced.

Who threw the rock and left the menacing message? Jake, retaliating after their argument? Natalie, Ethan's ruthless sister? Someone from Big Agriculture, bent on silencing his environmental campaign? Each sinister possibility multiplied, surpassing the last.

Samantha's eyes burned from fatigue and unshed tears as she stared at the ceiling. She felt unmoored, cast adrift in a sea of suspicion. Whoever stalked her, whatever their motive, one thing was evident - they meant business. And they struck at the heart of her sanctuary.

It was a long while before fitful sleep found her, slumber haunted by half-glimpsed shadows and phantom whispers of breaking glass.

Chapter 11

Samantha tossed and turned in her sleep, her slumber haunted by shadowy threats and the phantom whispers of breaking glass. When she finally opened her eyes, a pale morning light was already filtering through the shattered remnants of her bedroom window.

She laid still, reliving the previous night's events. The rock, the menacing message, the gnawing uncertainty of who was behind it. Her mouth was dry, her head pounding in time with her racing heart.

Pushing herself upright, Samantha winced at the wave of dizziness and nausea. She felt drained, hollowed, as if the mere act of breathing was an immense effort. But she couldn't afford to wallow, to surrender to her fears and doubts. The stakes were too high.

With leaden steps, she made her way downstairs to the kitchen, the hallways gaping and empty. A note on the counter confirmed Delores was out running errands, leaving Samantha alone with her hunger and her demons.

She rummaged through the cabinets, assembling a meager breakfast from the scattered remnants. A stale granola bar, a bruised apple, dregs of milk sloshing in the carton. She ate robotically, more from habit than any sense of appetite.

As she finished the last sip of milk, her eyes locked onto the knife block. Sudden awareness prickled along her skin, raising goosebumps in its wake.

The knife block on Delores' kitchen counter was a cheerful shade of yellow, the wood worn soft with age and use. Samantha Brewer ran a finger over the empty slot, a frown tugging at her lips.

There was a knife missing. A chef's knife, if she remembered correctly. Slender, sharp, perfect for slicing through tender flesh.

Like the flesh of a certain idealistic organic farmer.

Samantha's stomach turned, a sour taste flooding her mouth. She couldn't believe she was even entertaining the thought. Delores, her own mother, a killer? It was ridiculous. It was absolutely insane.

But doubt had taken root, and now it wouldn't let her rest. The crime scene photos haunted her, especially the image of Ethan's body splayed in the dirt, with a gaping wound in his chest. According to the coroner, the blade was thin and razor-sharp. The knife a cook might wield with practiced ease.

A cook like Delores, who'd spent her whole life feeding the hungry mouths of Willow Creek.

Samantha shook her head, trying to dislodge the traitorous thought. She was grasping at straws, seeing patterns where none existed. Countless reasons could explain the knife's absence. It might be lost, broken, or simply misplaced in the jumbled chaos of Delores' kitchen.

But as she turned to leave, a flash of color caught her eye. On the fridge, a tacky magnet held a faded Polaroid. She had seen this photo countless times, as it had a permanent place on the fridge, but something caught her attention. A much younger Delores, her hair a riot of dark curls, her smile wide and carefree. And beside her, a gangly teenage boy with laughing green eyes.

Ethan.

Samantha plucked the photo from the fridge, her heart hammering in her chest. They were at the county fair, the garish lights of the midway twinkling in the background. Ethan was holding up a rectangular box, his face split in a triumphant grin.

With a jolt, Samantha remembered the stories about young Ethan. The ring toss booth, the one Ethan had dragged her to every year, determined to win the grand prize. A set of fancy kitchen knives, imported from Japan.

He'd finally done it the summer he turned sixteen. Spent every dime of his allowance, but he'd walked away with that set of knives, so proud you'd think he'd won the lottery.

He'd given it to Delores, Samantha recalled. Presented it to her with a flourish, like a knight laying his sword at the feet of his queen. Delores had laughed, ruffling his hair with affectionate exasperation.

"What should I do with these, silly boy? Stab someone?"

The words echoed in Samantha's mind, a mocking refrain. She gazed at the photo and then the knife block on the counter, pondering. She eyed the photo again at the way Delores' eyes crinkled with mirth, a string of pearls gleaming at her throat.

Pearls. Something niggled at the back of Samantha's mind, a half-forgotten detail from the case files. Natalie had mentioned a necklace, hadn't she? A gift from her husband. She wore it during the murder, but it disappeared from the crime scene and was never located.

Could it be? Samantha squinted at the grainy image, trying to make out the details. The pearls looked old, luminous in the fading light. The thing a grieving sister might cling to, a symbol of happier times.

Certainty was crucial for her. She wondered if the pieces she saw were real, or just figments of an overtaxed imagination. She slipped the photo into her pocket and headed for the door, her mind already racing ahead to her next move.

Natalie's house was a squat, nondescript ranch on the outskirts of town, a secondary property she owned besides her luxury condo in town. The lawn was overly perfect and the curtains unduly drawn tight. Samantha rang the bell, shifting from foot to foot as she waited for an answer.

The door swung open, revealing Natalie's pinched, wary face. "Samantha. What a surprise."

Samantha pasted on a smile, hoping it looked more convincing than it felt. "Natalie, hi. I'm sorry to drop by unannounced. But I was hoping I could ask you a few more questions about Ethan."

Natalie's eyes narrowed, her lips thinning to a slash. "I thought we'd already covered everything. Multiple times, in fact."

"I know, and I apologize for the inconvenience. But there's just one minor detail I wanted to clarify." Samantha took a deep breath, steeling herself. "The pearl necklace. The one your husband gave you. Do you remember when you last saw it?"

Natalie had a momentary stare, something flickering in her eyes. Then she inched back, gesturing for Samantha to enter.

"It was the night of the murder," she said, her voice flat. "I was wearing it when I went to confront Ethan, to talk some sense into him about the farm. But when I left, after we'd argued... it was gone."

Samantha's heart stuttered, a sick lurch in her chest. "Gone? What do you mean, gone?"

Natalie shrugged, a brittle little motion. "I mean gone. Vanished. I tore the house apart looking for it, but it was like it had never existed. Initially, I thought maybe it had fallen off during the argument, that the police had found it and forgotten to return it. But when I called the sheriff's office, they said they'd never seen it. It wasn't in any evidence logs.

She looked at Samantha, her gaze sharp and probing. "Why? What's this about? Do you know something about my necklace?"

Samantha swallowed hard, her mouth dry as bone. "I... I'm not sure. But I believe I may have a lead. I need some more time for confirmation.

Natalie's lips twisted, a bitter little smile. "Time. That's all anyone ever wants from me, with Ethan. Time for grieving, healing, releasing anger and resentment. Well, let me tell you something, Samantha.

Time doesn't heal a single cursed thing. It just scabs over the wound, until something comes along to rip it open again."

Samantha flinched, the raw pain in Natalie's voice hitting her like a slap. "I'm sorry, Natalie. I know this hasn't been easy for you. But I promise, I'm doing everything I can to find the truth. To get justice for Ethan."

"Justice." Natalie spat the word like poison. "What good is justice when my brother is rotting in the ground? When everything he built, everything he believed in, is crumbling to dust?"

She turned away, her shoulders rigid with tension. "Do what you have to do, Samantha. But don't expect me to thank you for it. There's no happy ending here, no matter what pretty lies you tell yourself."

Samantha left Natalie's house feeling hollowed out, scraped raw. The old wounds festered, the secrets and lies bubbled to the surface like pus. And at the center of it all, the spider in the web was Delores.

Her mother. The woman who'd raised her, loved her, taught her everything she knew about right and wrong. She was supposed to be her rock, her safe harbor in the storm.

However, if her suspicion was correct... if Delores had killed Ethan, had stolen that necklace and hidden it away like a guilty trophy... then everything Samantha thought she knew was a lie. A facade, crumbling to reveal the rot beneath.

She didn't want to believe it. Didn't want to face the awful, inescapable truth. But she couldn't run from it anymore. Couldn't deny that the cracks in her family's foundation were just hairline fractures, conveniently fixed and covered up.

No, this was a sinkhole, a gaping maw ready to swallow them all whole. And Samantha was the sole person capable of preventing it before it was too late.

Dinner was a tense affair between Samantha and Delores. Samantha pushed her food around, glancing at the pearls gleaming on her mother's neck.

As Delores served her famous peach cobbler, Samantha reached out, letting her fingers skim the smooth beads. "That's a beautiful piece. Don't think I've seen you wear it before."

Delores paused, giving the necklace a reflexive once-over. "It was my mother's," she said, regaining her composure. "An old family heirloom. I don't bring it out very often, but I thought... well, with everything that's happened, I wanted to feel close to her."

Her voice wavered, tears springing to her eyes. Samantha's heart clenched, a wave of doubt crashing over her. Maybe she was mistaken. Perhaps there was an innocent explanation for everything, a perfectly reasonable reason Delores had Natalie's necklace, why that knife was missing from the block.

But then, as if in slow motion, the necklace clasp released, the string of pearls scattering across the table like spilled marbles. Samantha watched, transfixed, as one bead rolled to a stop in front of her, gleaming dimly in the candlelight.

With shaking fingers, she picked it up, rolling it between her thumb and forefinger. It felt cool to the touch, with a subtle irregularity. Just like the ones in the photo, the ones Natalie had described.

The pearls that vanished from the murder scene without a trace.

Samantha's head snapped up, her gaze locking with Delores'. They shared a silent moment, their eyes locked in a battle of wills. Then slowly, deliberately, Samantha slipped the pearl into her pocket, never breaking eye contact.

"Oops," she said, her voice barely above a whisper. "Better be more careful with that, Mom. Wouldn't want to lose it again."

Delores' face drained of color, her lips trembling. But she said nothing, just dropped her gaze to her plate, her hands shaking as she gathered up the scattered beads.

Samantha excused herself from the table, mumbling something about a headache. She fled to her room, her heart pounding in her chest, the pearl burning a hole in her pocket.

It was crucial for her to have no doubts. She needed certainty, beyond a shadow of a doubt, that she wasn't imagining things. That the clues were real, and not from her desperate, grief-stricken mind.

With trembling fingers, she pulled out her phone, scrolling through her contacts until she found the one she was looking for. Sheriff Cooper's gruff voice filled her ear, tinny and distant.

"Samantha? What's going on? It's late."

"I know, Sheriff. And I'm sorry. But I need your help. I think... I think I know who killed Ethan. And I have evidence to prove it."

There was a long pause, followed by static crackling. Then, a sigh, heavy with weariness and resignation.

"Alright, Samantha. Let's hear it. But this better be good. I'm not in the mood for any more wild goose chases."

Samantha took a deep breath, steeling herself. "It's Delores, Sheriff. My mother. She did it. And I can prove it."

The words tasted like ash on her tongue, bitter and acrid. But they were the truth, the awful, inescapable truth. Now that she had spoken them, there was no retracting her words.

Despite her desire, it didn't matter.

The next few agonizing hours ticked by in slow motion for Samantha. She had laid it all out for Sheriff Cooper - the missing pearls, her mother's suspicious behavior, the growing sense that something was awry. But having those words hang in the air made it no less difficult to grapple with.

Her mother, her family, the very foundation she had built her life upon - all potentially compromised by one horrific act of violence. Samantha drifted between determination to uncover the truth and desperate bargaining that somehow, some way, she had gotten it all wrong.

But the cold, hard facts refused to be ignored. Within the hour, Sheriff Cooper's team had obtained a search warrant and descended on the Brewer home.

Samantha could only watch in numb trepidation as they ferried out evidence bags and boxes one by one. The bloody knife. The damning strands of pearls that had triggered her suspicions, now confirming her worst fears.

It was almost anticlimactic in the end. The search of Delores' room, the discovery of the bloody knife, the necklace hidden beneath the floorboards. Her mother's face crumpled, all the fight left of her as the cuffs clicked around her wrists.

With a trembling hand, Samantha extracted her mobile device and composed a message to her friend Jenny. Her fingers danced across the screen, conveying the unthinkable: "The Sheriff just arrested my mother, charging her with Ethan Green's murder. More details later." She gazed at the screen, her eyes brimming with disbelief, before resolutely tapping the send button, unleashing the devastating revelation into the digital ether.

Samantha watched the ordeal unfold like a spectator at her own life, numb and distant. She couldn't process it, couldn't make sense of the fact that the woman who'd tucked her in at night, who'd kissed her scraped knees and wiped her tears, was capable of such a monstrous act.

But the evidence didn't lie. And as the Sheriff and Delores sat in the interrogation room, her shoulders slumped and her eyes hollow, truth came spilling out in fits and starts.

"I didn't mean for it to happen," Delores whispered, her voice thin and reedy. "I never wanted to hurt Ethan. But he called me asking for money, a lot of money, to fund his grand plans for the farm."

She looked up at Samantha; her face a mask of anguish. "He wanted to turn Green Acres into some kind of educational center for sustainable agriculture. A noble vision, he said, but one that would require investing everything we had and more."

Delores shook her head slowly. "I couldn't allow that, Samantha. I had to protect what little financial security we had left after your father passed. Ethan's dreams were admirable, but ultimately impractical pipe dreams that would leave us destitute."

Her voice broke, a sob tearing from her throat. "But he just kept pushing and pushing, berating me for being closed-minded and unsupportive. He wanted me to bankroll his grand design, no matter the cost. And I... I just snapped. I grabbed the knife, and I..."

She trailed off, her eyes squeezing shut. Samantha's stomach turned, bile rising in her throat. She couldn't breathe, couldn't think past the roaring in her ears.

"How could you?" she whispered, her voice a broken rasp. "Why would you betray Ethan and our family like that? He was like a son to you, Mom. He loved you."

Delores' head snapped up, her eyes blazing with a sudden, fierce light. "I loved him too, Samantha. Ethan *was* like a son to me. But I had to protect our family's future, don't you see? I couldn't allow him to gamble away everything we had on one of his starry-eyed schemes."

Her jaw tensed. "I was trying to make him see reason, to not risk our financial security on an idealistic dream. That's what a mother does. That's what loyalty to your family means - keeping them from ruin, even when it's hardest."

Samantha shook her head, tears blurring her vision. "No, Mom. That's not loyalty. It's sheer madness. That's the kind of crazy logic that makes people into monsters."

She stood up, her legs shaking beneath her. "I hope it was worth it, Mom. I hope your precious legacy is worth the blood on your hands. Because you've lost everything else. You've lost me."

Samantha watched it all unfold like a spectator in her own life, numb and distant. Unfathomable! Her rock of support turned into a perpetrator of a heinous act.

But the evidence was irrefutable. The weight of Delores' confession hung like a shroud; it blanketed the room in silence. For Samantha, it was the silence of shattered illusions, of the fragile lies that had once framed her world crumbling to dust.

She gazed at her mother, this woman she had idolized yet now regarded as a stranger, and felt something viciously cold take root in her heart. Disgust, certainly. Anger and betrayal, as potent as venom. But most of all, an endless, yawning chasm of loss and disillusionment.

Only then, perhaps, could we grasp justice amid the ashes. Only then could we momentarily quiet the screaming voices of grief.

With that grim resolution fortifying her, Samantha turned and walked out into the night, the ghost of her childhood finally laid to rest.

Chapter 12

As dawn broke, the front page of the Willow Creek Gazette blazed with the latest developments, capturing the town's attention with its bold headlines.

Flash Report: Arrest Made in Connection to Ethan Green's Murder

By Jennifer Mack, Willow Creek Gazette

WILLOW CREEK, IA — In a sudden and shocking turn of events, an arrest has been made in connection to the murder of beloved local farmer Ethan Green. Local law enforcement confirmed the arrest late last night but have not yet released the suspect's name or any specific details.

Ethan Green, 52, son of the late Kenneth and Evelyn Green, was found dead on his Green Acres Farm several weeks ago. Green had taken over the family farm after his parents' passing and was known for his dedication to organic farming practices. Since his death, the investigation has been ongoing, with Sheriff Emmet Cooper leading the effort.

"We have taken a person into custody based on compelling evidence," Sheriff Cooper said in a brief statement. "However, the investigation is still active, and we're working hard to gather all the necessary information."

The community of Willow Creek has been on edge since Green's untimely death and is now grappling with the implications of this latest development.

More details will be provided as they become available. Stay tuned to the Willow Creek Gazette for continuous updates on this developing story.

Note: As this story is still unfolding, we urge the community to remain patient and respect the privacy of all families involved.

The day after the news flash, Sam noticed the change in the town. The capture of the murderer brought relief and eased people's tension. However, they speculated quietly about who the killer could be. The following day, shocking news hit the papers.

Breaking News: Local Widow Arrested for Murder of Ethan Green

By Jennifer Mack, Willow Creek Gazette

WILLOW CREEK, IA — In a shocking development, local authorities have arrested Delores Brewer, 68, in connection with the murder of Ethan Green, a prominent organic farmer in Willow Creek.

Green, 52, was found dead on his property, Green Acres Farm, several weeks ago. The son of longtime Willow Creek residents Kenneth and Evelyn Green, Ethan had become a well-known figure in the community for his innovative organic farming practices and environmental advocacy.

"Evidence collected during our investigation has led us to arrest Ms. Brewer in connection with Mr. Green's death," Sheriff Emmet Cooper stated at yesterday's press briefing. "While the investigation is ongoing, we had sufficient grounds to take her into custody. We continue to gather and analyze information related to this case."

The arrest has sent shockwaves through Willow Creek, as Delores Brewer was a respected member of the community and Ethan Green's lifelong neighbor. Her daughter, Samantha Brewer, a true-crime podcaster, played a pivotal role in revealing the evidence that led to her mother's arrest. Samantha Brewer's investigation into her childhood friend's death has exposed unsettling details that are now at the center of the legal proceedings.

While officials have not disclosed specific details about the evidence leading to Brewer's arrest, sources close to the investigation suggest that key information was uncovered at the suspect's residence and continue to seek a motive.

"This is an incredibly challenging time for everyone involved, especially the families of the victim and the accused," Sheriff Cooper remarked. "We ask that the community remains patient as the investigation continues, and we will offer further updates as more information is uncovered."

Currently, Delores Brewer remains in custody as the investigation proceeds. The once tranquil town of Willow Creek faces a period of uncertainty and introspection, grappling with the reality of this profound betrayal within their community.

Stay tuned for more updates on this developing story. For continuous coverage, visit us online at www.willowcreekgazette.com.

Later that week, Delores' interview came up. The sheriff's detective teams finished their follow-up investigations considering the fresh evidence recovered from Delores' closet.

Samantha's heart thudded against her rib cage as she watched Delores through the one-way mirror. Her mother sat ramrod straight in the interrogation room, her hands cuffed and resting on the scuffed metal table. She looked small, somehow diminished in the harsh fluorescent light. But her eyes still glinted with that familiar, steely resolve.

The door creaked open and Sheriff Cooper stepped into the observation room, his weathered face grave. He nodded to Samantha, taking in her hollow expression, the shadows beneath her eyes.

"You doing alright?" His voice was a low rumble, laced with gruff concern.

Samantha started, as if snapping from a trance. She managed a tight nod. "As well as expected, I suppose. Just... go on and get it over with."

Cooper's mustache twitched, a rueful shake of his head. "You know how these types operate, Samantha. They'll try every trick in the book to muddy the waters, deflect blame, reframe their crimes as somehow justified." His jaw tensed. "Best prepare yourself for her to spin a new web of lies and excuses."

"I know." Samantha's voice was adamant, tinged with a fragile strength. "I must see this through, Sheriff. I owe Ethan that much, at least."

"Alrighty then. But remember, no matter what she says in there... it doesn't change who you are. You're not defined by your mother's sins."

The Sheriff's words hung in the air like a weighted talisman—both a sobering caution and a fragile lifeline.

Cooper turned toward the interrogation room door, his hand resting on the tarnished knob. But then he paused, his shoulders squaring as if under a sudden, invisible burden. Pivoting back to face Samantha, his lined features softened with a rare sincerity.

"I should've said this sooner, but... you cracked this whole mess wide open, Sam. Delores might've gotten clean away with it if not for your tenacity."

Samantha blinked, her throat constricting as a wave of conflicting emotions washed over her. Hearing those words from the gruff, no-nonsense Sheriff carried an unexpected weight. A begrudging validation of the countless hours she'd poured into her investigation, the risks she'd taken—both physical and emotional.

"I... well, it's like you said," she managed in a tight murmur. "I owed that much to Ethan, at least. Thank you, Sheriff."

Her gaze flicked past Cooper, through the observation window at her mother's rigid silhouette beyond the unforgiving glass. A strangled breath whistled between Samantha's lips as the tattered remnants of her childhood illusions threatened to unravel entirely.

Cooper seemed to read the turmoil whirling beneath her stoic veneer. He offered a solemn nod, as if in wordless affirmation of the profound violation she must be feeling. Mother and daughter, bound by blood... yet a universe of deception lay between them.

"I'll give you a minute." His voice was low, thick with the gritty weight of experience. "Then we'll get the truth from her, no matter how ugly."

With that, he turned and walked out through the door. Samantha stood alone, only the accusatory glare of the two-way mirror and the phantom murmurs of the past haunting her thoughts.

Cooper strode into the interrogation room, the door slamming shut behind him with a clang that reverberated in Samantha's chest.

"Delores Brewer," Cooper intoned, his weathered frame sinking into the creaking chair across from the elderly woman. His piercing gaze met her unwavering stare, an unspoken challenge passing between them. "You've been read your rights?"

Delores inclined her head in an almost regal gesture, her gray curls framing her face like a crown. "I have." The words fell from her lips with measured precision, betraying no hint of emotion.

Cooper's brow furrowed as he leaned forward, the harsh interrogation lighting casting sharp shadows across his rugged features. "And you understand the charges against you? Murder in the first degree, for the death of Ethan Green?"

A flicker of something - a fleeting glimpse of pain, guilt, or perhaps even regret - flashed across Delores' face, her warm brown eyes darkening with a storm of unspoken turmoil. But the moment passed, and Delores swiftly reclaimed her composure, settling an impenetrable mask of calm over her weathered countenance.

"I understand perfectly, Sheriff." Her voice, though steady, held a faint tremor, betraying the turmoil that lurked beneath the surface. "But I'm afraid there's been a terrible misunderstanding."

Cooper leaned back in his chair, the vinyl squeaking. "Is that so? Then, by all means, enlighten me."

Delores' hands clenched the worn wooden table, her knuckles blanching white with the force of her grip. "I... I was there that night, yes. But not to harm Ethan. I could never..." Her voice wavered, a glimmer of unshed tears shimmering in her warm, brown eyes. "I loved that boy like he was my own flesh and blood."

Behind the two-way mirror, Samantha felt the air catch in her lungs, a sudden weight pressing against her chest. Her mother's words, painfully familiar, mirrored the very thoughts that had been consuming Samantha's mind these past agonizing weeks. The ache of irreparable loss, the gutting realization that Ethan was gone forever - it was a pain they now shared, even if Delores had a twisted, overbearing way of expressing it.

Cooper seemed unmoved by Delores' display of emotion. He tossed a manila folder onto the table, crime scene photos spilling out in gory Technicolor.

"Then explain this," he said, jabbing a finger at Ethan's lifeless face. "Explain how he ended up with stab wounds in his chest, lying in a pool of his own blood in those cabbage fields he loved so much."

Delores flinched, her gaze skittering away from the gruesome images. "I... I didn't mean for it to happen. We argued, yes. About his plans, about the direction his life was taking."

She shook her head slowly. Ethan had approached me about a week before that tragic night, seeking a significant amount of money to finance his ambitious idea of converting Green Acres into an educational hub focused on sustainable agriculture.

Delores' expression hardened. "I told him it was madness - putting my family's financial future at risk on such an impractical pipe dream. I begged him to reconsider, to be more pragmatic about my limited resources."

Her hands twisted anxiously in her lap. "But you know how single-minded Ethan could be. Once he got an idea in his head, he was relentless. He accused me of being closed-minded, of stifling his noble ambitions out of greed and fear."

Samantha's heart clenched at her mother's words. Though she acknowledged Ethan's passion could make him stubborn, it was difficult to fathom him lashing out so cruelly at Delores.

"So you killed him over a disagreement about money?" Cooper's voice was flat. "Took his life because he wanted to chase an idealistic vision you didn't approve of?"

Delores' trembling hands flew to her mouth, her eyes wide and wild with panic. "No, no, it wasn't supposed to happen this way!" she cried, her voice quavering. "Sheriff, please believe me - it was an accident, a horrible and awful accident!"

Her shoulders slumped as she confessed. "The argument, it became heated. We said hurtful things. And then... then he lunged at me in a blind rage. I had no choice but to defend myself."

Delores' gaze dropped as tears welled in her eyes. "It was an accident, a terrible accident. I never meant to take his life. I only wanted to protect myself and the little I had left...

Samantha felt her heart fracture at her mother's anguished words. Though Delores' account was undoubtedly self-serving, there remained a kernel of truth - her desperation to safeguard their family, however misguided.

Yet even that flicker of sympathy couldn't extinguish the roiling tempest in Samantha's gut. Ethan was dead, his vibrant life snuffed out in an instant of blind fury. And at her own mother's hand, no less. The betrayal hollowed her from the inside out.

How could Delores allow things to devolve so catastrophically? Hadn't she seen the depth of Ethan's passion, the righteousness of his convictions? Samantha's fists clenched, nails biting into her palms.

Sheriff Cooper regarded her in stony silence for a moment, his brow furrowed with skepticism. "If it was an accident, then why didn't you call us?" he pressed, his tone hardening. "What did you do then?"

Delores' shoulders slumped, her matronly facade crumbling as she confessed, "I... I was scared. There was so much blood, and Ethan wasn't moving. I just... I went home." Tears welled in her puffy, reddened eyes as she choked out, "I cried for Ethan."

The Sheriff's voice escalated, cutting through the thick tension in the room. "You went straight home? Didn't bother to call anyone, to get help?" He shook his head, his expression etched with disappointment. "Delores, your story of self-defense just doesn't add up. You know it just like I do.

The Sheriff leaned forward, folding his hands on the table. "Which brings me to another concerning pattern of behavior, Mrs. Brewer. The threats, the acts of intimidation aimed at your own daughter while she was investigating this case."

Delores visibly stiffened, but Cooper pressed on relentlessly.

"The slashed tires on her car. The attempted run-off-road incident. And let's not forget the rock thrown through her bedroom window with that lovely little warning note."

He shook his grizzled head. "Those don't seem like the actions of someone just trying to protect their family's interests, now do they? No, that's the mark of someone desperate to bury the truth by any means necessary, even if it means turning those same violent intentions on their own kin."

Cooper fixed her with a piercing stare. "So I have to ask you straight out - did you hire someone to terrorize and frighten your daughter into dropping this investigation? Or did you play a bigger part in that campaign of intimidation?"

Delores flinched at Cooper's accusation, her shoulders tensing. For a moment, she seemed to wrestle with herself, weighing denial against confession.

Finally, she lifted her gaze, her expression a mask of mingled defiance and shame. "I... may have taken some measures to discourage Samantha's investigation. But I never intended actual harm!"

The words tumbled out in a desperate rush. "I was only trying to protect my family, to protect the truth from being twisted and exploited. Can't you understand that, Sheriff?"

In the observation room, Samantha felt bile rise in her throat. Her own mother, orchestrating acts of violence and terror against her? It was perverse, a total inversion of everything a parent should be.

Delores pressed on, pleading for understanding. "I knew if Samantha kept digging, kept poking around in ancient history, it would only lead to more pain for all of us. I had to make her stop, by any means necessary."

Samantha's fists clenched until her nails bit into her palms. The betrayal sliced through her like shards of jagged glass, each new revelation another agonizing twist of the knife.

First, my own mother's hand in Ethan's death - an act of unconscionable violence. Now, her willingness to unleash that same malice and depravity on me, all in the name of preserving her web of secrets and lies.

When would the revelations end? What fresh hell awaited, what new depths could her reality possibly sink? Samantha felt unmoored, cast adrift on a churning sea of darkness and despair.

As Cooper's interrogation bored into Delores, the former illusion of her mother's love and loyalty crumbled into ash and ruin. Samantha could only watch, feeling hollowed and numb, as he systematically unearthed the full, monstrous truth.

"Any means necessary? Really? That's pretty low, Delores. More like you were protecting you and not your only family."

Delores sat in silence, her gaze downcast, as the weight of her actions settled heavily upon her. The Sheriff's stern scrutiny bore into her, stripping away her veneer of innocence and laying bare the troubling truth she had sought to conceal.

The room was thick with tension as Cooper's words hung in the air, their weight bearing down on Delores like an unbearable burden. Samantha watched, her heart pounding, as her mother's expression shifted from defiance to resigned acceptance of the truth.

Cooper's bushy brow furrowed as he leaned forward, the creaking of his chair punctuating the pregnant silence. "Come on, Delores. Why'd you really kill him?" His voice took on a sharper edge. "Not wanting to loan Ethan money justified taking his life? Or did you give him the cash already, and wanted it back?"

Delores' gaze dropped to the glossy crime scene photo, the gruesome image of Ethan's lifeless body sending a shiver down Samantha's spine. "I told you, it was self-defense," she insisted, a tremor in her voice. "He forced my hand. I didn't mean for it to happen, but he gave me no choice!"

Cooper scoffed, leaning back in his chair. "Well, ain't that a coinky-dink, Delores? Of course it's his fault." His mustache twitched with derision. "C'mon, seriously? You expect me to buy that load of organic horse-pucky?"

The crinkle of the manila envelope cut through the charged atmosphere as he retrieved another photograph. "Maybe this'll jog your memory, Mrs. Brewer." He slid the image across the table with a flat thunk of finality.

Delores' eyes widened as she stared at the familiar pearl necklace, the weight of its history etched into the weathered lines of her face. "Why yes. It's my necklace, the one my mother gave to me. I'd recognize it anywhere. It's been in the Wilkins family for over a hundred years."

Leaning forward, Cooper's gaze bore into Delores, his voice low and measured. "We recovered this necklace from your house with the bloody Japanese knife, the one with your fingerprints all over it, which, by the way, is covered with Ethan's blood. We ran the DNA. But why would you put your valuable family heirloom under the floorboards of your closet, along with the murder weapon?"

Delores opened her mouth to protest, but the Sheriff's soft chuckle cut her off. "Oh, I believe she gave it to you, no doubt. But it still isn't yours."

Samantha watched, her mind racing, as the pieces of the puzzle fell into place. Just when she thought the depravity of her mother's actions couldn't descend any further into darkness, another chasm opened beneath her feet.

The necklace, the financial struggles, the tangled web of lies and secrets her mother had already confessed to weaving - it all coalesced into a fresh disintegration of any remaining illusion of Delores' innocence or justification. Ethan's murder, once merely a horrific reality, now gained an additional dimension of premeditation and coverup.

"Well, that just makes good ol' common sense, Mrs. Brewer, like hay in a barn come winter," Cooper continued, his voice laced with a somber understanding. "You pawned it about 25 years ago at Price's Pawn over in Mason City, after Richard died. According to old lady Lois Price's sworn statement, you said you needed the money and hoped to buy it back. But that didn't happen, did it?"

Delores shook her head, her lips trembling as the weight of her actions settled heavily upon her. Samantha could see the anguish in her mother's eyes as she realized that the necklace, a symbol of her family's strength and resilience, was lost to her forever.

The room fell silent, save for the soft sniffles escaping Delores' trembling lips as she faced the devastating truth. Samantha's heart ached for her mother, the layers of deception and desperation that had driven her to this tragic end blurring the lines between victim and perpetrator. In the tense stillness, Samantha grappled with the complex emotions threatening to consume her.

"Here's where your story unravels, Mrs. Brewer. And by cracky, you almost got away with it." Cooper's voice cut through the charged atmosphere, his words carrying a weight that seemed to press down on them all. "After you killed Ethan, you didn't go straight home as you suggested. You went back to the house to retrieve his Japanese knife from the kitchen. And that's when you saw it - something you would recognize anywhere."

Delores sat rigidly, her fingers fidgeting in her lap as Cooper continued, "You spotted the broken necklace on the floor, and your overwhelming greed to finally reclaim that cherished heirloom overtook you. You scooped up the scattered pearls, that precious symbol of your family's legacy, and took them home with you, arranging Ethan's body to appear as a suicide on your way home."

The sheriff shifted in his creaking chair, his gaze unwavering. "The necklace was the crucial piece of evidence against you, Mrs. Brewer. You almost got away with it lock, stock and barrel, but that telling clue exposed the truth."

Delores stiffened, her defiant eyes flashing. "You can't prove that. You're trying to frame me for something I didn't do. I told you, it was an accident."

"Inspect the photo, Mrs. Brewer." Cooper slid the image across the table, its glossy surface reflecting the harsh fluorescent lights. "You certainly know your necklace well. I'm sure you noticed something missing."

Delores leaned in, her brow furrowing as she scrutinized the image. Suddenly, her eyes widened in realization. "There's a pearl missing! What did you do with it? Is this some kind of cruel joke?"

"No, Mrs. Brewer. It's no joke." Cooper extracted another photograph, this one showcasing a solitary pearl alongside a ruler. "Do you recognize this?"

Delores stared at the image, her lips trembling. "Yes, it's the missing pearl. Why did you separate it from the rest? Are you trying to frame me?"

"Not at all, Mrs. Brewer." Cooper's voice remained calm, his gaze unwavering. "Natalie Sandoval has provided a sworn statement. She was at the farmhouse that night, engaged in a heated argument with Ethan about the farm's financial troubles. Amid the argument, the worn clasp released, and the pearls scattered on the floor. Natalie, consumed by her anger, simply left them there and departed."

He paused, allowing the gravity of his words to sink in. "It was your daughter Samantha who brought the necklace to our attention. We searched the farmhouse again and found a single pearl hidden under the stove. This ties you to the scene, Mrs. Brewer. You didn't go straight home that night. You went to his kitchen, retrieved Ethan's knife, and left with the necklace as well."

Delores fidgeted in her chair, her composure crumbling.

Cooper's voice rose, the accusation ringing out. "You planted Ethan's own knife on his body, didn't you? You killed him in cold blood, over a meaningless argument, just because he defied you. Fess up, Mrs. Brewer. You murdered him for nothing more than your own greed and need for control."

Delores' countenance shifted abruptly, her features hardening as a veil of defiance fell over her expression. "No, no, that's not the way it happened. It was so incredibly important, but Ethan just wouldn't listen." Her voice quivered with a mixture of desperation and indignation, her hands trembling slightly as she gripped the arms of her chair. The warm, maternal facade crumbled, revealing the depth of her conviction and the unwavering belief that she had been in the right, no matter the cost.

Delores drew in a shuddering breath, her body visibly tensing as she steeled herself for the admission. "Ethan, he... he said he knew the truth. About Richard. About Samantha." Her voice wavered, thick with emotion. "He'd found an old letter, you see. One I thought I'd burned decades ago."

Samantha felt a frown tug at her brow, confusion and unease swirling in the pit of her stomach. The truth about her father? What is she talking about now? What in the world did Ethan stumble upon that pushed someone to commit murder?

Beside her, Cooper leaned forward, bracing his elbows on the table as he fixed Delores with a piercing stare. "What truth, Delores? What in tarnation was in that letter?" he pressed, his tone laced with a mixture of trepidation and resolve.

For a long, agonizing moment, Delores remained silent, her gaze distant and haunted, as if she were peering into the depths of a painful past. Then, slowly, painfully, the words spilled from her trembling lips, each syllable weighted with a lifetime of regret and anguish.

The room fell silent, a heavy blanket of tension smothering the air. Delores' trembling lips parted, and the words spilled forth like a torrent of anguish. Delores' weathered features crumpled with the weight of a lifetime's worth of regrets, the shame etched into every line of her face. "Richard and I... we had our troubles that first year of our marriage. He was always working, always distant. Ken needed help at Green Acres, and Richard felt obligated to help his neighbor with that project. I was so young, so desperate for love, and longed for our marriage to succeed." She swallowed hard, her throat constricting with the painful memories. "He started coming home late more and more often that year..."

The air grew thick with tension, the silence a suffocating blanket that threatened to smother them both. Delores inhaled, quivering, bracing herself to reveal the final, devastating truth. "I found out, Sheriff. He betrayed our vows, my husband betrayed our vows... and nine months later, along came Ethan."

The world tilted on its axis, Samantha's vision tunneling as the realization struck her like a physical blow. Ethan... their neighbor

Ethan... could it be true? She choked, her lungs seizing in her chest. If what her mother was saying was real, then that would mean... "Ethan was my half-brother," she whispered, the words like ashes on her tongue, a bitter truth that threatened to shatter the very foundations of her reality. "My own flesh and blood."

Cooper went statue-still, the air vacated from his lungs. His weathered features slackened, mouth hanging slightly ajar as the tectonic implications of Delores' confession echoed through the interrogation room. For an endless, suspended moment, he could only gape at her, utterly stunned into speechlessness.

The gruff lawman's composure cracked as he wrestled with the ancestral bombshell. Trembling fingers rose to rake through his thinning hair as he huffed out a strained, disbelieving breath. "Jumping Judas... you're saying..." His voice cracked, trailing off into pensive silence as the truth solidified.

Cooper's bushy brows knitted together, the craggy lines of his face etched in anguish and reproach. When he finally found his voice, it was hushed with stunned gravity. "Delores... you murdered your daughter's own flesh and blood? Her own kin?" His gaze bored into her, chiseled eyes glistening with a sheen of unshed moisture. "I didn't think even you were capable of that level of depravity."

Delores nodded miserably. Fresh tears carved glistening tracks down her weathered cheeks. "We had argued over the phone for days. He said Samantha deserved to know. I faced him that night, in the fields. He planned to reveal everything to Samantha, shattering our universe with the truth. I begged him not to, told him it would destroy her. But he wouldn't listen."

She lifted her gaze to Cooper; her weathered features etched with desperation. "I never intended to take his life, Sheriff. I swear it on all that I hold sacred." Her voice trembled, the words escaping in a ragged breath. "We struggled, and in that moment of panic, I grabbed the knife to frighten him and make him see reason."

A gut-wrenching sob tore from her throat, raw and anguished. "But he lunged at me, and I..." Delores shook her head, fresh tears carving glistening tracks down her aged cheeks. "It was an accident, a horrible, unforgivable accident. And the weight of it will haunt me until my dying day."

Samantha squeezed her eyes shut, hot tears spilling down her own face as she fought to process the unthinkable. Her mother, a murderer. Her friend and neighbor, her brother in all but name. The web of secrets and buried lies unraveling in one shattering instant, leaving her reeling in the wake of this devastating revelation.

She didn't remember standing, didn't remember wrenching open the interrogation room door. But instantly she was there, staring down at Delores with a maelstrom of emotions churning in her gut.

"How could you?" she whispered, her voice broken and raw. "How could you keep this from me? From Ethan?"

Anguish and desperation were displayed on Delores' face as she looked up at her. "Samantha, please. I was trying to protect you, to spare you the pain..."

"Spare me?" A cracked, mirthless laugh. "You murdered my brother, Mother. Ripped him away from me before I even knew what he was. There's no coming back from that."

Cooper stood, laying a hand on her shoulder. "Samantha, I know this is a lot to process. But the law needs to finish it now."

Samantha shrugged him off, blood roaring in her ears. "The law? What good is the law when it can't bring Ethan back? When it can't give me the years I lost with him, the bond we could have shared?"

She turned to Delores, fury and grief warring in her chest. "I hope you rot in here, Mother. I hope you spend every day of the rest of your miserable life haunted by what you did. Because I know I will be."

With that, she turned abruptly, fleeing through the station doors and out into the blinding sunlight. She ran until her lungs burned and her legs gave out, collapsing onto the sun-warm earth of Ethan's fields.

She lay there for a long time, salt tears mingling with the rich, loamy soil. The same soil that had cradled her brother's body, that had drunk his blood. The soil he had fought so hard to preserve, to nurture with his sweat and his passion.

At that moment, Samantha understood her task. Ethan was gone, but his dream didn't have to die with him. She would take up his mantle, continue his fight. She'd pour her own blood and tears into this land until it bloomed with life and purpose once more.

For Ethan. For the brother she'd never known, and the future they'd never get to share. She would make this place a legacy, a living testament to his ideals.

And perhaps, just maybe... it would be enough to quiet the screaming in her soul. To fill the yawning chasm his loss had carved out of her heart.

Samantha pushed herself to her feet, squaring her shoulders against the weight of grief and regret. Work awaited, a new chapter beckoned.

And she'd be the author, crafting a legacy from the ashes of buried lies - one powerful truth at a time.

Epilogue

With the world already swept up in the frenetic pace of the digital age, the New Year arrived without excitement. The transition from 2014 to 2015 brought about a significant change in Samantha Brewer's life. The media hype surrounding the Orion test flight and NASA's ambitious plans for deep space exploration had captivated the public's attention in the previous months, but now, as the dust settled and the world moved on, Samantha confronted a new reality - one in which her mother was behind bars and her own future was a blank page waiting to be written.

For Samantha Brewer, the anticlimactic passage of time brought a strange sense of disconnection, a feeling untethered from the world around her. The media hype and hysteria of the preceding months had been a welcome distraction from the turmoil of her personal life, the still-raw wounds of betrayal and loss that haunted her waking hours.

She stepped out into the crisp morning air, her boots crunching against the frost-dusted grass as she made her way across the barnyard. The familiar sights and scents of Green Acres Farm enveloped her like a warm embrace, carrying with them a flood of memories that threatened to overwhelm her fragile composure. A tractor in the distant field pulled a loaded wagon in its wake.

She couldn't help but be drawn inexorably to the weathered tractor parked beside the machine shed, with its faded green paint peeling and rust streaked. A ghost of a smile tugged at the corners of her mouth as she approached, her fingers trailing reverently along the sun-warmed metal of the hood.

Closing her eyes, Samantha allowed the memory to wash over her, vivid and alive...

"Sammie! Over here, come look at this."

Nine-year-old Samantha whirled at the sound of Ethan's voice, her bare feet kicking up puffs of dust as she scampered across the sunbaked field toward him. He was crouched beside an ancient, rusted-out tractor, its once-glossy green paint chipped and faded to a sickly olive hue.

Ethan straightened as she approached, his brow furrowed beneath the brim of his tattered baseball cap. "Looks like the old girl has given up on me again," he sighed, swiping a calloused hand across his brow.

Samantha frowned, peering at the decrepit machine with a critical eye. "Can't you just buy a new one, Ethan?" she asked, her small voice laced with exasperation. "This one's always breaking down."

A rich chuckle rumbled from Ethan's broad chest as he shook his head, his green eyes crinkling with amusement. "It's not that simple, Sammie," he replied, beckoning her closer with a wave of his hand. "This tractor has been a part of the farm for a long time. It's got history, and it's my job to take care of it."

He motioned for her to join him as he swung open the tractor's rust-streaked hood; the hinges protesting with a shrill creak. "See, when something's broken, you don't just throw it away," Ethan explained, his deep voice taking on the gentle, patient cadence he reserved solely for her. "You try to fix it, to understand what's wrong and make it right."

Samantha watched, transfixed, as Ethan's hands deftly navigated the tangle of greasy machinery, his fingers plucking and prodding with the ease of long practice. "But what if you can't fix it?" she couldn't help but ask, her young mind already grappling with the complexities of Ethan's philosophy.

Ethan paused, his piercing gaze finding hers as a warm smile tugged at the corners of his mouth. "Then you learn from it," he replied, straightening to his full height and beckoning her closer still. "You take what you can, and you use that knowledge to improve things in the future."

The memory flickered and faded, leaving Samantha adrift in the present once more. She drew in a shuddering breath, her fingers tightening around the worn metal of the tractor's hood, as a fresh wave of determination washed over her. With one final, lingering caress of the battered tractor, Samantha turned and made her way back across the barnyard to the house, her strides purposeful and unhurried. She left a note on the table saying, "Went to Mitchellville. Be back this evening."

With a heavy heart and a sense of grim determination, she climbed into her car and pointed it towards the Iowa Correctional Institution for Women in Mitchellville, the prison where Delores Brewer now called home.

Samantha's heart hammered against her ribcage as she stepped into the cold, stark visitor's room. The fluorescent lights buzzed overhead, casting a sickly pallor over the cinder block walls and the hunched figure sitting at the center table.

Delores Brewer lifted her head, and Samantha's breath caught in her throat. Her mother looked like a faded photocopy of herself, all washed out colors and blurred edges. This hollow-eyed shell had replaced the vibrant, indomitable force of nature she'd once been, diminishing her by the weight of her sins.

Samantha hesitated; her feet rooted to the dingy linoleum. It had been months since she'd last laid eyes on her mother, though she had visited a few times in the intervening period. The betrayal, the loss, the shattering realization that Ethan - her neighbor, her confidant, her friend - had been something more, something infinitely precious and forever lost to her, still weighed heavily upon her with each return.

The pain of it all still thrummed through her veins like a discordant chord, but beneath it, a new melody was emerging. A song of understanding, of forgiveness, of moving forward even when the road ahead was pitted with shadow and doubt.

With a deep breath, Samantha crossed the room and slid into the chair opposite Delores. Her mother flinched, bracing for the onslaught of recrimination and rage she'd grown accustomed to from her daughter's rare, terse visits. But Samantha gazed at her, long and hard, her hazel eyes inscrutable behind the glint of her glasses.

The silence stretched between them, taut as a garrote wire. Delores' hands twisted in her lap, her fingers gnarled and liver-spotted, the nails bitten to the quick. Samantha noted with a pang the absence of her mother's signature red polish, the color as much a part of her as the gray in her hair or the laugh lines around her mouth.

Finally, Samantha spoke, her voice rusty from disuse. "I've missed you, Mama."

The words hung in the air, soft and fragile as spun glass. Delores' head snapped up, her eyes wide and disbelieving. For a moment, she just stared at Samantha, her mouth working silently. Then, like a dam bursting, the tears came, great heaving sobs that shook her narrow shoulders and echoed off the bare walls.

"Oh, Sammie," she choked out, the old nickname slipping from her lips like a prayer. "I'm sorry. I'm so sorry, baby girl. For everything. For Ethan, for the lies, for... for all of it."

Instinctively, Samantha reached across the table, taking her mother's trembling hands in her own. The skin was thin as tissue paper, the bones as delicate as a bird's. The touch was a lifeline, a fragile thread to the woman who once meant everything to Samantha.

"What you did..." Samantha began, her throat tight with emotion. "It was unforgivable. Monstrous, even. But I understand now that it came from a place of misguided love." She paused, letting the weight of her words sink in. "I'm not ready to forget, Mama. But I am ready to forgive."

Delores' grip tightened on Samantha's fingers, her eyes shining with a mix of hope and disbelief. "Truly? After all I've done, all the pain I've caused... you can find it in your heart to forgive me?"

Samantha nodded, a small, sad smile playing at the corners of her mouth. "Ethan taught me that, you know. The power of forgiveness, of second chances. He always saw the best in others, despite their inability to see it themselves." She swallowed hard, blinking back the sting of tears. "I want to honor his memory, Mama. Not only by solving his case, but also by living like him. With compassion, with grace, with an open heart."

Delores let out a shuddering breath, her head bowing under the weight of her daughter's words. "I don't deserve you, Sammy. I never have. But I swear, I'll spend the rest of my days trying to be worthy of this gift you've given me."

Samantha squeezed her mother's hands, a silent acknowledgement of the long, hard road ahead. For both of them.

"There's something else," she said, leaning forward with a new intensity. "I've been thinking a lot about the farm, about Ethan's vision for it. And I've decided... I'm going to make it a reality."

Delores blinked, surprise and confusion warring on her face. "The farm? But I thought... with Ethan gone, and Natalie contesting his claim to the property..."

Samantha's expression hardened, a muscle ticking in her jaw. "Natalie and I... we've come to terms, for Ethan's sake. She's agreed to not fight the will's directives regarding Green Acres' ownership."

She exhaled slowly, as if bracing herself. "But there's a condition. Natalie insists I honor Ethan's vision by operating Green Acres itself as a sustainable agriculture model - his principles put into practice on the land he fought so hard to preserve."

Samantha held up a hand to forestall any interruption. "The land he fought for, not the Brewer property or the Emersons'. This is about his legacy, his life's work."

Samantha felt the weight of responsibility settle onto her shoulders, a muscle ticking in her jaw as she fully committed herself to the path ahead. But her expression was resolute, eyes blazing doggedly to honor her brother's legacy.

Her eyes bored into Delores, a world of unspoken subtext simmering beneath the surface. "It's the only way she'll allow me to proceed unopposed as the executor of Ethan's estate and final wishes for Green Acres."

Delores' eyes flickered with pride, the first genuine spark of life Samantha had seen since entering the room. "That's... that's wonderful, honey. I know it won't be easy, but if anyone can do it, it's you." She smiled then, a wobbly, tear-stained thing. From a young age, you were always the strong one. Stubborn as a mule and twice as smart."

Samantha huffed out a laugh, the sound rusty and unfamiliar in the sterile air. "Wonder where I got that from," she teased, a ghost of their old banter rising to the surface.

In a momentary pause, their eyes met, a delicate understanding emerging. Then, the buzzer sounded, harsh and grating, signaling the end of their time together.

Samantha reluctantly stood up, her hands slipping from her mother's grasp. "I have to go," she whispered, an apology in her eyes. "But I'll be back, Mama. I promise."

Delores nodded, tears streaming freely down her cheeks. "I know you will, baby girl. And I'll be here, counting the days until I see your face again."

With a final, fierce hug, Samantha turned and walked out of the visitor's room, her head held high and her heart lighter than it had been in months. The road ahead was long and winding, full of pitfalls and uncertainties. But for the first time in a long time, she felt hope stirring in her chest.

THE SUMMER SUN WAS just beginning to dip below the horizon as Samantha pulled up to the old Brewer farmhouse, painting the sky in streaks of orange and pink. She sat briefly, idling the engine, taking in the sight of the place that had greatly influenced her life.

The porch sagged a little more than she remembered, the paint peeling in long, curling strips. Nevertheless, the bones retained their strength and durability. With a little love, a little elbow grease, it could regain its beauty.

Just like her. Just like the tangled web of lies and secrets that had bound her family for so long, slowly revealing truth and forgiveness.

Samantha climbed out of the car, her boots crunching on the gravel drive. She could almost hear Ethan's voice on the breeze, could almost see his lanky form ambling towards her, a crooked grin on his weathered face.

"Welcome home, chickadee," he seemed to whisper, the words curling around her like a benediction.

Samantha smiled, a genuine smile, the first in longer than she could remember. She looked out over the fields, the neat rows of crops stretching towards the horizon, the rich, dark earth waiting to be coaxed into new life.

It wouldn't be easy, this new chapter she was writing. There would be long days and longer nights, sweat, blood and tears blending in the soil. But it would be worth it, every blister and bruise, every aching muscle and dirt-caked nail.

Because this was her legacy now, her birthright. It's not about lies, secrets, and wounds, but about land, family, and unbreakable bonds of love and resilience that carried them through dark times.

She rolled up her sleeves, her eyes fixed on the horizon. It was time to get to work.

SAMANTHA EASED OFF the rumbling 4-wheeler, her boots crunching on the gravel driveway. A kaleidoscope of autumn hues swirled through the air as a brisk wind whistled its autumnal melody. The familiar routine of retrieving the mail offered a welcome respite from the emotional turmoil swirling within her. She strode towards the weathered mailbox, its faded red paint chipped and peeling, a remnant of simpler times.

The familiar routine of retrieving the mail offered a welcome respite from the emotional turmoil swirling within her. She strode towards the weathered mailbox, its faded red paint chipped and peeling, a remnant of simpler times.

Swinging open the creaky mailbox door, she extracted the stack of envelopes and flyers, rifling through them with practiced nonchalance. Bills, catalogs, the usual assortment of junk mail—nothing out of the ordinary. Until her gaze snagged on the sterile medical letterhead, her name emblazoned across the envelope in bold typeface: "Genetic Analysis Results."

A razor-thin slice of white space separated that fateful envelope from the rest of the stack. Samantha's fingers instinctively pried it apart, her heart thudding with a sudden, inexplicable urgency.

Flashes of her confrontation with Delores over Ethan's paternity detonated in her mind's eye. The anguished disbelief etched on her mother's face as the truth spilled forth. The knife's edge of uncertainty about her own identity, slicing deeper with each revelation.

This envelope, this innocuous slip of paper, held the power to reforge her ancestral truth, to rewrite the very fabric of her existence.

Samantha's grip tightened around the envelope, her knuckles whitening. A barrage of memories assaulted her—the warmth of

Ethan's embrace as a child, the shared laughter over secret jokes, the bond forged in the soil of the Green family farm. Who was Ethan? A carefully constructed illusion woven by her mother's deception?

Her throat constricted, and she swallowed hard, pocketing the envelope with a heavy heart. She would open it later, when she was prepared to confront the truth it contained, whatever that may be.

The dusty path crunched beneath the tires as Samantha guided the 4-wheeler back towards the farmhouse. Her gaze swept over the familiar landscape, drinking in the sights that had become as comforting as an old friend's embrace.

The red barn stood tall and proud, its weathered boards a tapestry of faded hues, each chip and crack a testament to its enduring strength. The silo jutted skyward like a sentinel, watching over the neatly tended fields that rolled out in verdant waves.

A figure emerged from the barn's yawning doorway, and Samantha's heart skipped a beat. Jake, his coveralls streaked with grease and sweat, squinted against the late afternoon sun. A slow smile tugged at the corners of his mouth as he caught sight of her approaching.

Samantha killed the engine, the sudden silence enveloping them like a warm blanket. She hopped off the 4-wheeler, boots crunching on the packed earth, and made her way towards Jake.

"Afternoon, darlin'," he drawled, that familiar lopsided grin sending a flutter through her chest. "I was wonderin' when you'd get back from runnin' your errands."

Samantha arched an eyebrow, her lips quirking in a playful smirk. "Errands? Is that what we're calling it now?" She held up the stack of mail, waving it in front of his face. "Pretty sure this counts as actual work, mister."

Jake chuckled, low and rumbling, as he wiped his hands on a grease-stained rag. "If you say so, boss lady."

Before Samantha could muster a retort, he closed the distance between them, calloused fingers brushing her cheek with a tenderness that still caught her breath. Their lips met in a lingering kiss, soft and unhurried, a balm for the weary soul.

As they parted, Jake's gaze dropped to the envelope poking out from the stack of mail, his brow furrowing. "That what I think it is?"

Samantha followed his line of sight, her heart stuttering in her chest. The sterile medical letterhead seemed to mock her with its bland formality. She nodded, her voice gone in a flash.

Jake's arm snaked around her waist, drawing her close. His lips grazed her temple in a gentle kiss. "Whatever it says, we'll face it together," he murmured. "You and me, remember? Samantha Jean Emerson?"

A tremulous smile tugged at Samantha's lips as she leaned into his solid warmth. "You and me," she echoed, a comforting phrase against the storm of uncertainty brewing on the horizon.

Later, as the last rays of sun painted the sky in brushstrokes of crimson and gold, Samantha sat alone in the old farmhouse. Dust motes danced in the slanting beams of light that filtered through the window, casting the room in a dreamlike haze.

With trembling fingers, she tore open the envelope, the crisp tear echoing in the silence like a gunshot. A single sheet of paper slipped free, its clinical formatting at stark odds with the existential weight it carried.

Samantha's eyes skimmed the impersonal text, the detached recitation of genetic markers and probabilities:

Genetic Analysis Results:

Sample G417-A (paternal source)

Sample G417-B (subject)

...

Probability of paternal relationship between samples: 99.9999%

The evidence she'd longed for emerged in perfect clarity: 99.9999% paternal match between her and Ethan Green.

The paper slipped from her suddenly numb fingers, fluttering to the floor in a silent surrender. Ethan's face swam before her mind's eye, those warm green eyes crinkling with shared laughter, that crooked grin a beacon of home and acceptance.

Stumbling towards the window, Samantha gazed out over the fields that had shaped and sheltered generations of her family. The endless furrows stretched towards the horizon, rich earth waiting to nurture new life into being.

With a shuddering breath, she stooped and plucked a seedling from the tray on the sill, cradling it in her palm like a newborn babe. This tender shoot, this fragile promise of growth and renewal... it was her birthright, her legacy inscribed in the very soil that had given her life.

Ethan's dream was in her blood, flowing through her veins with every thrumming heartbeat. As sure as the sun rises each day, that dream will flourish and blossom anew.

THE END.

Endorsements

Praise for *Fertile Ground for Murder*

"★★★★ Loved it! ☺ A sleuth podcaster seeking justice in a murder case...yes please! I highly recommend this story!"

"*Fertile Ground for Murder* is a well-developed and thought-out story with murder theories that keep you on your toes. Just when you think you have the case solved, **Stella Sinclair** throws you off your tracks and leads you in another direction. This psychological thriller kept my attention all the way through."

- Lauren Jones, M.Ed., Avid Reader and Book Reviewer

★★★★★ If you enjoy uncovering secrets in a place where even the cornfields seem to whisper their disapproval, (*Fertile Ground for Murder*) will keep you hooked until the last page.

- Literary Titan

★★★★★ "...gripping and moving story with a fast pace and plenty of surprises along the way."

- Booksdown

★★★★★ I strongly recommend *Fertile Ground for Murder* to anyone who enjoys mysteries with strong characters and social issues.

- K.C. Finn for Readers' Favorite

★★★★★ Just when you think you've figured it out, there's a twist that makes you rethink everything.

- Progress Wings

"★★★★★ A thrilling murder mystery that will keep you on the edge of your seat and the pages turning. Stella Sinclair and Steven Nimocks do an amazing job at bringing this thriller to life. You can easily imagine the events of this wonderful story thanks to the vivid imagery and amazing design each chapter has. Thank you both for an amazing story."

- Jacob Midyette, Troy University

Also by Stella Sinclaire

Thieves in Velvet
The Silent Sonata
Fertile Ground for Murder
Les Racines du Meurtre

Also by Steven Nimocks

Hidden in Plain Hue
Schizophrenia
The Elusive Isle
Thieves in Velvet
Desperate Remedies
Shattered Trust
The Last Librarian
Fertile Ground for Murder
Confiance Brisée
Les Racines du Meurtre
The Smart House
The Balance of Fear
The Core Directive
Help Desk

Watch for more at https://shortstorylovers.com/Steven-A-Nimocks4.

About the Author

Stella Sinclaire and **Steven Nimocks** form a formidable literary partnership, blending their unique talents to create mesmerizing stories that captivate readers worldwide. **Stella**, an acclaimed mystery author, brings her mastery of dark family secrets, psychological twists, and moral complexities to their collaborative works. Raised in the English countryside, her connection to mysteries hidden within stately manors infuses their narratives with an authentic, atmospheric touch. With a Master's degree in English Literature and years of teaching experience, Stella's clever plotting and nuanced character studies have earned her critical acclaim in the mystery genre.

Steven complements this partnership with his exquisite touch of refinement and precision in storytelling. His diverse cultural encounters, including time spent in Germany and Austria, add a rich, global perspective to their joint creations. Steven's skill in crafting narratives that fuse imagination and reality perfectly dovetails with Stella's intricate mystery-weaving abilities.

Together, Stella and Steven offer readers an enchanting literary voyage that spans continents and genres. Their collaborative works combine the atmospheric intrigue of English manor mysteries with the cosmopolitan flair of European landscapes. Readers can expect stories that not only challenge and enthrall but also provide a captivating fusion of traditional mystery elements and contemporary, globally-influenced narratives.

From the solace of Stella's study in her family manor to the inspiration drawn from Steven's international experiences, this dynamic duo continues to push the boundaries of storytelling. Their partnership promises to deliver tales that are both rooted in the rich tradition of mystery writing and expanded by a worldly, imaginative touch. Embark on a journey with **Stella Sinclaire** and **Steven Nimocks**, and prepare to lose yourself in a world where secrets, cultural diversity, and masterful storytelling converge.

Read more at https://www.shortstorylovers.com/Steven-A-Nimocks4.

About the Publisher

Three Notch Publishing is a boutique publishing house founded by **Steven Nimocks**, **Lyam Lockwood**, and **Stella Sinclaire**. With a shared passion for storytelling, they are dedicated to bringing unique and compelling voices to readers worldwide. Though their focus is primarily on **fiction**, ranging from mystery and suspense to literary fiction, they are also open to working on **non-fiction** projects that align with their vision.

At Three Notch, the team believes in cultivating an intimate relationship with both authors and readers, ensuring that each project receives the attention and care it deserves. Their collaborative approach allows for the development of stories that push boundaries, evoke emotion, and leave a lasting impact.

With years of combined experience in literature, writing, and publishing, the partners of Three Notch are committed to supporting authors through every stage of the publishing process, from manuscript development to final publication. Their goal is to help talented writers find their audience and create works that resonate.

For inquiries, submissions, or further information, **Three Notch Publishing** can be reached via email at: **threenotch@ml1.net**